Darkness Of Nature

Brian L Alford

Published in 2018 by FeedARead.com Publishing

A CIP catalogue record for this title is available from the British Library.

Our destiny is in the hands of others and events beyond our control. Life is fragile and simple events can have profound effects.

Chance and fortune are hard task masters. Circumstances can lead us to a place we do not want to be and from which we cannot escape.

Is any of us capable of coping especially when something dark, real or imagined, is lurking in the background?

~ 1 ~

It was all my fault. For as long as I could remember I had wanted to see big game in the wild. I don't really know why but it was one of the things on the bucket list I kept in my head. Not that I approved of such lists. They just seem to be an excuse for people to do ridiculous things. Its as if being on a bucket list renders something unwarranted credibility. I know its stupid but would you deny a dying man his last wish? We are all dying. Its just a matter of when so get on with the list before its too late.

Not committing the list to writing meant I could change it at will. I had to admit it was a form of cowardice. If something could not be achieved, or cost too much, or I could not be bothered it could be removed from the list. Seeing wild life in Africa was set firmly in the list. It was achievable if I could persuade the family. Surely they would indulge me such a simple request?

Unfortunately no one in the family agreed with this particular idea of a holiday. The children loved the beach, the sea and ready access to junk food. Jane liked nothing better than to lie round the pool reading and doing very little. When pushed as a compromise she would settle for lying on the beach just so long as the kids left her in peace.

Raising two boisterous kids and holding down a part time job took its toll and Jane preferred to relax and recharge her batteries. A holiday was her chance to discharge her child minding duties and let me take them on. She would dump them on me, wish me luck and march off to the pool book in hand. If I was lucky I would get a friendly wave and beaming smile as she trudged away. I would then be abandoned with the expectant faces of two small children.

In truth I was happy to comply since it was an opportunity for me to gain a better understanding of our children and they of me. Perhaps they would see someone other than the grumpy father who came home miserable from work each day and was always telling them off for being naughty. It was a chance to get up to some mischief together. How far could the children drag me into trouble? How far was I prepared to let them before grumpiness took over again? Time spent with them was as much of an adventure for me as it was for them. They could challenge me to do outrageous things and I could see how little I could get away with.

As a contrast to the stresses of the corporate world I always welcomed the chance to spend time with the children. They did not play politics with me or try to be one up on me, or knife me in the back. I had no reason to maintain my guard. They had no ulterior motives or hidden agendas. Their pleasures in life were far more simple and much easier for me to accommodate than the sharks that dwelt in the corporate world. Looking after them required physical energy not the mental energy that work demanded and drained from me. Time with them was fulfilling not mentally destructive. They were after all the main reason I endured such an unattractive job.

I could rationalise my longing for an active holiday. I wanted adventure, a break from our mechanical family life. Life passed too quickly. I could see the children growing rapidly before my eyes and was missing so much. Work earned the money for me to provide for a good upbringing for the children, but it was an upbringing I was seeing very little of. I wanted to build memories both we and the children could remember fondly in the future. It would be a way of measuring our lives together beyond the daily drudgery. I admitted that our day to day lives were not exactly scintillating and wanted to add some adventure to enhance them. I argued that a safari adventure was for the benefit of the children but I knew that it was more a selfish desire.

I was a salesman and used all my expertise to negotiate. If I could sell software to tough corporations under difficult circumstances; my family were surely a simpler challenge. I simply had to sell and idea. I did not need to extract money from them or draw up complicated agreements. Simple promises were enough. We did not need expensive lawyers.

After much argument and persuasion the family had agreed and so we headed for Kenya. I confess I had been a little underhand beguiling the children with stories of how they were going to meet elephants face to face and play with monkeys. Tom our four year old boy was particularly excited at the prospect of seeing lions. For days afterwards he ran round the house roaring and pouncing on everyone.

It was a cheap ploy but seemed harmless enough at the time. In truth I had later to admit it was the sort of manipulation I practised at work but vowed never to use on my family. I did not sell the end product, the trip itself, but the prospect of seeing wild animals. It was a bit like selling a cake by selling the virtues of the cherries on the topping. The exact contents of the cake were a little vague. I did not really know what we could expect in Kenya.

As the children's excitement grew Jane had surrendered and agreed. Though my conscience told me I had been a little unfair on Jane I felt a mild sense of victory. I was however determined to make sure she enjoyed the holiday too I would look to provide sufficient opportunity for her to enjoy as much as possible of the rest and relaxation she craved. I had booked a resort that had a large swimming pool with ample space to crash out and lie around. I was confident I had every angle covered for everyone to enjoy the holiday. My conscience became clearer and was eased even more as their acceptance grew.

I had researched all the problems with bugs and insects and we took every recommended precaution. We were particularly careful with the kids since I had read children tended to be more susceptible to many things adults could shake off more easily. Had I mentioned the injections I am sure they would have been less enthusiastic about playing with monkeys, but the die had been cast. They had told all their friends so they were stuck. They had dug themselves into a hole. Young children hate to climb down even more than adults. Adults can rationalise a climb down; children are not so self deluding. Also, peer pressure can be a compelling force and children can be so cruel. How could they face their friends if the trip was cancelled? Would they be accused of lying?

When on the third day of the trip Jane showed me the red spot on her arm it seemed such a harmless bite. It was one of many our bodies were covered with. As careful as were were the damn bugs always managed to find a way through. The copious amounts of chemicals we sprayed our bodies with seemed to make no difference. I even joked that it seemed to attract them rather than repel.

But this one tiny bite was different, it started small and grew angrier almost by the hour. It was like some creature growing in size and ferocity. As we were to find out later the mosquito that bit her had apparently been carrying a rare, possibly new strain of Encephalitis. Within a day of contracting the virus Jane became tired and nauseous.

When dizzy spells were causing her to faint without warning the resort manager arranged for me to take her to the local hospital. On reflection the deep look of concern on his face should have been a warning. He lived with these bugs, why should he have been so concerned about such an everyday event?

In contrast at first the doctors who examined her were not overly worried. They treated many such cases each year and most patients recovered but two days later Jane slowly slipped into a coma. I could tell from the stern demeanour of the doctors that this was more serious and their concern grew quickly as we sat by her bedside hour after hour.

A procession of doctors came and examined Jane. I was unsure as to whether the heightened attention Jane was receiving was a good or bad thing. Was her condition so unusual it elicited such curiosity? Did all the doctors want to see this new phenomenon?

It was a fairly simple matter to re-assure Angela and Tom as ten and four year olds. Mummy was not well and sleeping. She would be better soon. Why is it parents exploit the trust and naivety of their children so shamelessly? For me there was no re-assurance as the expression on the face of her doctor told of his ever deepening concern. His words provided no comfort to contradict the worried look on his face.

"Your wife's illness is a puzzle. It is not unusual for a patient with Encephalitis to slip into a coma if it is untreated, but in your wife's case she has received all the correct treatment. This should not have happened."

I paused letting his words sink in. Doctors always seem so confident and assured. His lack of either was worrying. Where were the reassuring words about not worrying? It was becoming clear that he was lost as to what was happening to Jane. I needed to understand what was on his mind.

"These patients that slip into a coma, do they recover?"

He pursed his lips considering his reply. I had obviously asked a difficult question. Perhaps he was trying to decide whether to be honest with me or simply spout some comforting platitude. He opted for the former.

"I will not lie to you, some do, many do not. But as I said, those that do not recover usually have not received treatment or receive it too late. The treatment your wife is receiving should be effective. I would expect her to recover. Perhaps it just needs more time to work. Her vital signs seem alright. To all intents and purposes she is just in a very deep sleep. The brain often switches off when the body is healing. All its effort is focused on healing. I understand it is difficult but we must be patient and wait and see. Your wife is young and strong. She is putting up a good fight."

There was a distinct lack of conviction is his voice. It was as if he was exploring options out loud rather than giving an authoritative explanation. His words did not sound convincing but they did not completely display lost hope, more like frustration. Struggling to find a distraction from the awkward conversation the doctor nodded at the children.

"They are very well behaved. We get some real monsters in here sometimes. I do wonder about the behaviour of children today."

I looked at Angela and Tom who were sitting quietly staring at Jane. Were they watching for signs of mummy waking as daddy had promised? Seeing the distant look in their eyes and the sadness on their faces I realised that this was not the best place for them to spend so much time. Outside the weather continued to be fine and there was much to do to distract them back at the resort.

"I think it best if I take them away from here. Will you call me the moment there is any change?"

"Of course. We have the number of the hotel and your mobile number. I promise someone will call as soon as there is any change in her condition whatever... well you know. Let's hope for the best. I'm sure everything will be fine."

Again his comments were distinctly lacking in conviction but I was not in a position to challenge him.

There was a strange mixture of reluctance and eagerness to leave in the children. They wanted to stay but felt ill at ease, but their continued trust in their father persuaded them we should go. We were going back to the resort to let Mummy have some quiet to get better. It made sense to them and they agreed. Was their faith in me well placed?

By the third day as Jane continued her deep sleep I had decided I needed to tell a few people about her condition. I needed to prepare them for the worst whilst desperately trying to ignore this possibility myself. When I broke the news to Jane's parents they were calm and accepting. Both were fatalists. Jane had been through a lot in her life. They had nursed her through childhood illness. They had seen her recover from a serious car crash. They knew Jane to be a survivor. There was a relaxed confidence about them which I avoided dispelling. I knew it was serious but did not want to cause alarm.

A week went by and despite repeated assurances from family and friends that I was not to blame and that it was just bad luck, I was inconsolable. Seeing Jane lying motionless and unable to help made it worse. Jane was losing weight and the enforced inactivity was taking its toll on her appearance. She had gone from looking healthy but asleep to looking desperately ill. Her face was pale and drawn as if the life was ebbing away from it.

Continued uncertainty nagged away at me and my reassurances to the children were losing credibility. Children can be very sensitive and perhaps I was sounding less convincing. The look on my face and the tone in my voice were probably telling them much more than my words of comfort. I was not a great liar. It was one of my stubborn principles to always tell the truth so the pretence I was attempting did not come naturally. In truth I did not know how to lie and look convincing, but silence would have been worse so I continued the charade. I convinced myself I was protecting the children. Lying was acceptable if it was for the greater good.

~ 2 ~

It was just past three o'clock in the morning when the telephone rang. It interrupted a strange dream I was having. A shadowy figure was following me trying to steal the children. It was not quite a pied piper figure, someone far more sinister. They say that all dreams have a basis in reality and this particular dream caused me some concern. Where had the idea come from? The repeated ringing overwhelmed the thought and it quickly vanished like all dreams tend to in the light of reality. As the brain becomes swamped with the sensual information from the real world the fantasy fades. With the disappearance of the dream the vague feeling of dread also faded. As disturbing as the dream had been it had gone. The real world was beckoning in the shape of the irritating telephone ringing.

Picking up the receiver I croaked a soft greeting. My brain was not yet completely awake so I spoke as if answering a call at work. I had done it hundreds of times.

"Robinson. Thanks for calling."

A voice on the phone sounded familiar.

"Mister Robinson, I have some good news. Your wife is awake and talking. She has drunk some water and eaten a little food."

It was the doctor in charge of Jane's case. Though I had been waiting and hoping for this news it took me by surprise. I shook my head to check this was not also a dream. My silence caused the doctor some concern.

"Mister Robinson? Are you still there?"

"Yes, sorry. I am still half asleep. That is great news thanks. Should I come in now or later?"

"Everything seems to be an effort for her so I expect your wife to drift off to sleep again. I suggest you leave it a few hours, 'till say eight o'clock when the hospital is a little more awake. We don't really like night-time visitors unless its an emergency and I am just about to take your wife off the critical list. She will therefore no longer be on open visiting. We are much less concerned about her. I will also be going home and will be back in tomorrow morning so we can talk then."

His comment struck me hard. Jane was off the critical list. This was about the first time the doctor had admitted just how serious Jane's condition was. It did not come much worse than open visiting. Didn't that mean the patient was not expected to live?

"Can I bring the children?"

"Of course, but I need a quick word with you before they go in."

"Is there something wrong?"

"Nothing to worry about. I will explain tomorrow."

Did this last comment lack conviction? Over the past few days I had lost trust in what the doctor said. Perhaps I was being too sensitive. He probably just wanted to warn me not to let the kids excite Jane too much. A debate started to rage in my head. They were less concerned but still concerned never-the-less. What did that mean? Uncertainty breeds uncertainty.

Saying good-bye and putting the phone down I got out of bed and walked around the room. I could not stop the manic debate running through my brain. Confused thoughts went through my mind. Perhaps we could go home and get back to normal. It would soon be time for Angela to go back to school. I could stop paying out a fortune for the hotel. The helpful manager was even more helpful in relieving me of more money. Would Jane be able to travel? What should I tell the kids?

I sat in a chair and let my brain do its worse with its rambling thoughts. Jane's illness had changed so much about the way I saw life. My innate certainty about the course of life had become tenuous and I was finding myself less able to make decisions. It was not that I was blaming Jane, rather that her illness had started to expose a deficiency in myself of which I had been unaware. When life ran smoothly I was competent and in control but when something went wrong I struggled. I always saw too many options and became indecisive. I feared making the wrong decisions and in consequence the fear came true. They say indecision is decisive. It was certainly true in my case.

It was six o'clock when I decided to wake the children and get them ready. By the time they had finished messing about the hotel would be serving breakfast. In the strange few hours I had sat awake I had decided I would simply tell them we were visiting Mummy and make no mention of her recovery until I had seen the doctor. Suppose Jane had had a relapse and slipped back into a coma? I was not sure how they would handle the disappointment. It would also weaken still further their trust in anything I said. The lies I had been telling them were starting to haunt me.

The short drive to the hospital was completed in silence. Did the kids suspect something was going on or was it just the early awakening? I wondered whether I should have said something to them. In the absence of anything better perhaps they were suspecting the worst.

As we approached Jane's room I could see the doctor inside examining the various monitors and scribbling on something. Telling the children to wait outside I entered the room. Shaking my hand vigorously the doctor spoke with cautious enthusiasm.

"Glad to meet you again under better circumstances. I just wanted to warn you that when you talk to her she does not respond immediately. It's strange, as if she is hearing something for the first time and taking time to assess it. I suspect the virus has affected her brain."

"Affected how?"

"It may be brain damage but we are not yet sure."

It was like a lightening bolt hitting me. He had said it in such a cold, matter of fact manner. But he had said it with more certainty than he had spoken for days. He seemed more sure of himself with bad news.

"Brain damage? How serious is it?"

"Oh don't worry. She has not become vegetative or anything like that, quite the opposite. She is very alert. But it looks like her brain is functioning differently."

"You are not making any sense."

"If the virus has damaged her brain then it will take some time to re-adjust. I have heard of cases where the patient has effectively become a new person."

None of this was making sense and I needed more clarity.

"I don't understand what you are saying. How can someone become a different person?"

"It is possible that the brain will build new neural pathways to bypass the damage. We do not use a lot of our brain. Pathways could be built connecting to parts of the brain that have never been used before, or possibly used only very little. In this case it is impossible to predict the effect. It could mean that she behaves differently. But don't worry. I'm sure things will settle down. The illness was a traumatic shock and her brain may just be taking time to recover. It shut down whilst she was in a coma; its now just starting to wake up again. You know what its like when you first wake up."

I nodded in agreement. It had happened to me earlier when he had called.

"I do."

"I am doing my early morning round and must go and see my other patients. I will come back a bit later to see how you are getting on. And if you have any more questions I can answer them then."

"Thank you. Could I ask you to send my children in as you pass them."

With a nod and a smile the doctor left the room. Seconds later Angela came in leading Tom by the hand.

All this time Jane had been sleeping but the noise of the children's arrival woke her. Tom could not do anything quietly, even keep quiet.

As I stood at the bed side Jane looked up at me and frowned. I touched her right arm reassuringly. At least I thought it was reassuring but Jane withdrew her arm immediately. I tried not to feel rejected but it was a disturbing moment. She did not seem to recognise me or was I being too sensitive?

I stood for a few minutes whilst Jane studied me intently. Heeding the doctor's caution I was not rushing her but letting her sort things out in her own mind. As the silence between us continued I became conscious of the children. It was strange, Tom and Angela stood at the end of the bed reluctant to come closer to Jane. They kept looking at her as if she were a stranger. Their faces looked strained. Were they showing a hint of being scared? Could they look beyond the familiar exterior and see something unfamiliar inside? I beckoned them to come forward to the side of the bed. Angela spoke with a quiet and uncertain voice.

"Are you feeling better now Mummy?"

Jane frowned and looked intensely at Angela. An odd and unfamiliar voice challenged her coldly.

"Who are you?"

Angela burst into tears and backed away. Grabbing my hand she looked up at me pleadingly.

"Can we go now Daddy?"

Seeing Angela's distress Tom also backed away and came close to me. As the children clung on to me I froze with uncertainty. What should I do? Looking at Jane's cold unemotional face I decided it would be for the best if I took the children away again. They could come back when Jane was feeling better, whatever that meant.

Outside I could see the Doctor sitting at the nurses station scribbling on some paperwork. Without looking up he sensed my approach. He gave me a quizzical look and spoke quietly.

"What do you think?"

"She does not seem to know who we are."

"You will need to give it time. I'm sure she will get her memory back. She has been through a very serious illness. When the brain is affected it can do some strange things but it usually sorts itself out. We never lose our memories but the retrieval mechanism can get damaged. I believe that is what happened in your wife's case. She needs time to adjust."

Again there was a less than convincing edge to his voice. Was he trying to convince me or himself? Or was he just speculating out loud again? I was increasingly suspicious that he was speaking for the sake of it. He was going through the motions and saying what he thought I wanted to hear. This angered me. I thought we had an understanding. I just wanted the truth. But it was becoming clear that he did not really know the truth. He was baffled and guessing. It was not so much medical science as medical guesswork.

Over the next two days I took Tom and Angela to see Jane regularly. Gradually Jane's coldness and hostility melted and she started to talk to them and call them by their names. There was even the odd smile as we talked about some of their antics, especially Tom's who managed to find trouble with ease. At one point he came into the room wearing a bed pan for a helmet and ran around pretending to sword fight. A nurse came in, glared at him and retrieved the bed pan.

But despite the apparent warmth Jane was showing there remained an uncomfortable distance. It was a different warmth, shallow and forced. The natural warmth and concern Jane had previously shown as a loving mother seemed to be missing. Now she was acting a part but acting poorly.

Three days later the doctor was satisfied that Jane had recovered physically and could be discharged. All tests showed that she was completely clear of the virus and whatever brain damage she had suffered was having no significant effect on her motor or cognitive skills. No mention was made of her mental state. This it would appear was not their concern. They had done their jobs making Jane physically better.

On hearing the news I organised our return home with an overwhelming sense of relief. Perhaps in the environment of our familiar home Jane would become more her old self. And I had to confess that looking after the children was taking its strain. Jane did it with such ease; for me it was a battle. I don't know where they found all the energy to keep going so boisterously all day. Tom's incredible ability to find trouble was very wearing. I was sure the nurse would be relieved that she would no longer need to keep chasing after Tom to recover the bed pans.

~ 3 ~

Preparations for going home were chaotic. Tom and Angela misbehaved and disrupted my packing. In my concern for Jane I had let them play on their own in the resort. Unsupervised they had found all manner of mischief. Tom had conjured up no end of trouble and it was unreasonable of me to expect Angela to look after him. Now I needed them to behave I realised I had loosened the reins a little too much. The result was fractious and bad tempered children with whom I needed to be much stricter than usual. Playing the heavy handed father only made them more difficult. I was clumsy at it and they resented it. Our relationship was built on negotiation and compromise not dictatorship. Though most of the compromise came from me I was accomplished at persuading them to my way of thinking.

Finally I had organised everything and the children had accepted that we were going home from what seemed to them like a permanent holiday. School and pre-school were beckoning but these were nowhere near as attractive as the resort.

They were not so sure about going home with what Tom called their 'new mummy' but it had to be done. I had to dissuade him from referring to 'weird mummy' especially within earshot of Jane. We had agreed on 'new mummy'.

For most of the journey home Jane slept. It was not the calm sleep of fatigue but a restless, disturbed sleep. On the plane she would occasionally wake with a start and look around with a confused almost frightened expression. Her eyes would scan the children and then me. Satisfied she would drift off to sleep again. It seemed that she had overcome her initial reaction to seeing us and now saw us as something familiar in unfamiliar surroundings. Surely that was progress? Though she did not talk to us and was still distant, she did at least seem to accept us. I was desperate for signs to be optimistic about her recovery. It was easy to rationalise the smallest signs but I was on the edge of delusional.

During the drive from the airport Jane stared out of the window blinking too regularly to be normal. It was as if she was blinking in disbelief at what she was seeing. A more likely explanation was that she was struggling to cope with the movement. If she were indeed having to relearn this would have been a new and confusing experience. Unfamiliar things were rushing past the car window too fast to be assimilated. Perhaps her brain was struggling to cope with the sensory overload.

On entering our house Jane hesitated in the hallway and looked around her. Standing stationary for several minutes whilst I lugged our cases in, she appeared to be trying to familiarise herself with the unknown. She did not recognise our home. Frequently looking at the children seeking something familiar she stood shaking slightly.

Assuming she was still tired and needed to rest I held her arm and gently showed her upstairs into our bedroom. Again she stood looking blankly with no hint of recognition registering on her face. Though I was worried I had been prepared by the doctors for just such a reaction. Her brain was still recovering. It might take time and we needed to be patient. Things might seem new to her but she had shown that she could adjust quickly. Her reaction was of submission rather than hostility.

Jane lay on the bed and fell asleep within seconds as if a switch had been turned off. I watched for a while curious to see how she would sleep. I had been warned by the doctor that Jane's sleeping pattern was disturbed. In hospital she tossed and turned and often broke out into a sweat. It played havoc with the monitors that kept a watch on her. She was also given to crying out and mumbling in her sleep. He said we should be prepared that she would sleep a lot. She would need to sleep at least ten hours a night and probably a few hours during the day.

Given all these problems the following day I decided that we should give Jane her own room and bed to sleep in. She could come and go whenever she felt the need to sleep. There was also the problem that I often worked late at night when the children had gone to bed. In her own room I would not disturb her when I came to bed.

At the time I was using the small room in the front of the house as a study. I decided we would clear this and move Tom into it. I could work downstairs once the children were in bed. Jane would sleep in Tom's room at the back of the house next to the bathroom and furthest from any noise.

My fears that the disruption would upset Tom were unfounded. He saw it all as a great adventure. As he loved to fiddle with everything he had been banned from my study. My study was a no-go area so it was exciting to be sleeping in it. What treasures would he find? I took great pains to remove anything I did not want him to touch. He was at that age where he would behave in my presence but took my absence to mean he could do whatever he wanted. He needed an external restraining influence since his own self restraint was still immature.

I took Jane's lack of objection to mean that she was amenable to the idea and after we had finished all the moving she spent most of the following day sleeping in what had been Tom's room. We had no need to disturb her. We had stocked the bedside cabinet with water and things to eat so that she could help herself whenever she felt the need.

The provisioning exercise made the children feel they were helping. Some of their suggestions were questionable but I went along with them to please them. Who eats mayonnaise, chocolate and cheese together? It was patronising but I still harboured concerns about the impact Jane's illness was having on them. It was important the children felt they were involved and helping.

As night approached on that second day I looked in on Jane. For several minutes I stood watching the restless woman. She constantly twitched and muttered almost inaudibly. It was uncomfortable to watch but at the same time fascinating. No wonder she was so tired if even in sleep she expended so much energy. She was calmer and less active when she was awake.

Hearing a noise I suddenly looked down to see two little heads between my legs also looking at Jane. Angela and Tom had joined me with their childish curiosity. Tom twisted his head to look up at me.

"Is Mummy alright?"

"Yes, she is asleep."

Angela was frowning and staring intently at Jane as she continued to twitch restlessly.

"Why is she doing that?"

"Do you mean the shaking? We all do it when we are asleep. Its because she is having a bad dream. Come on we must not disturb her. If she wakes up and sees you two monsters staring at her it might frighten her."

I shuffled backwards pushing the children behind me. They both giggled as they fell over and scurried off. I quickly looked back at Jane. To my relief I saw that we had not woken her. She had turned onto her side and the twitching had stopped. For now she would get some peaceful sleep. The monsters had left her. Her recovery could continue.

Later that evening I looked in on Jane again before retiring to bed. On entering her room I saw she was lying on her back with her eyes wide open apparently staring at the ceiling. Instinctively I looked up but saw nothing.

"Are you alright Jane?"

As I continued to look I realised that she was in a deep sleep. Though she was calm and lying completely still she was muttering. As I listened I realised she was having a conversation. It was like hearing someone on the telephone when you can only hear one side. It was an earnest and compulsive conversation. Whoever she was talking to was causing her some distress.

I debated whether to wake her but recalled a conversation with the Kenyan doctor. He had told me that Jane's brain would need time to adjust. He suggested that most of this adjustment would happen whilst Jane slept and that is why she would sleep a lot. This was the way it worked for all of us. Sleep was essential for the brain to process everything that had happened during the day. If everything was new for Jane then the adjustment need would be greater. Reluctantly I decided to let her sleep on.

Gradually over the next couple of weeks Jane's sleeping became more settled and less disturbed. She seemed less tired when awake and whatever conversation she had been having had come to a conclusion. I was buoyed by the thought that she was showing signs of recovery.

Though she was still a stranger to us we had comes to terms with her condition. She had even succumbed to the children's offering of mayonnaise and chocolate. To the revulsion of my taste buds I had been obliged to join in.

~ 4 ~

We had been home for just over two months and my concern was deepening. Jane had changed. Though she no longer treated us like people she had never met she seemed to lack any interest in life. Everything was an effort and too much trouble. Her sharp temper was something new and the smallest things annoyed her intensely. Every little thing would spark a bad reaction from her. I had never known her shout at the children but now she did it almost all of the time. She had become a stranger to us and not a particularly nice stranger. Our home was no longer filled with affection and comfort but anger and discontent. Jane roamed the house like some caged animal.

At first physically Jane looked the same but mentally and emotionally she was very different. But after a while even physically she started to change. Caring little for herself Jane was becoming a mess. Her hair was unkempt and unwashed. Her complexion was becoming pale and sickly due to lack of exercise, not eating properly and never going outside. When she walked around the house she shuffled as if her joints were stiffening. Not only had she changed mentally she was transforming into a different person physically. Was this the effect of the virus? Had it also affected her physically as well as mentally? Or was it her mental state causing a physical decline?

I recalled reading some research about the link between our personality and our physical appearance. At the time it had seemed barely credible but was I now seeing the truth of this? I puzzled long and hard without conclusion as the woman I knew slowly transformed into a wild stranger. This bad tempered wreck of a woman occupied my thoughts entirely. I did not exactly neglect the children but I did pay them less attention than I should. I was trying to protect them from this disturbed person we were living with.

Gradually the children were changing too. They were becoming more withdrawn and uncertain of themselves. Never sure of how Jane would react they were treading more carefully. Our bright outgoing children were becoming introspective and inward looking. The surety and security we had worked so hard to build around them was being eroded. Everyday things that used to interest and excite them now passed them by. They had no time for trivialities. There were bigger more important things to do. I realised that they were in fact becoming more and more like Jane. Their outlook on life was changing and they were losing their childhood.

I understood how they were struggling to cope with Jane. I too was finding it difficult. But it was particularly distressing that their attitude towards me was changing. They were becoming selfish and self centred quickly losing their tempers when something did not please them. Where once I could reason with them now they simply became obstinate and refused to listen. It was as if all our years of teaching them how to behave were being thrown away. They were copying the behaviour of their mother. Jane did not listen to me so why should they? Our behaviour as a family group was declining. I too was starting to shout at them as my frustration at their behaviour got the better of me. Tiredness was making me short tempered. The life I knew was slipping away and being replaced by something more uncomfortable.

Being younger Tom was less affected than Angela. He would sulk for a short while and then become his boisterous self again. Angela however was becoming permanently moody. She too was fast becoming a different person, almost a stranger. Of course children went through changes as they aged but usually these were gradual transitions that could be noticed. There was always a reasonable explanation for the change. The change in Angela was more sudden and dramatic.

I had to do something but what? For a fleeting instant the unthinkable thought crossed my mind that I needed to get the children away from Jane. Perhaps with her absence I could steer the kids back to normality. How had it come to this?

I decided to confront Jane. I knew it would be difficult because she would either ignore me or fly off into a temper. But I could not stand by and watch what was happening. I was losing them all, Jane and the children. They were turning into people I did not know.

Convinced things had not yet gone too far I knew I had to act quickly.

I caught Jane alone in the kitchen making herself a cup of tea. I had grown used to the fact that she no longer offered to make me one. In the three months since we had been home she had never shown me any consideration. She cared only for her own needs.

"Jane, I have to say this: you seem to have no patience with the children any more."

In a dismissive gesture Jane shrugged her shoulders.

"I never wanted kids."

It was a bolt from the blue.

"What?"

Jane looked at me with eyes that were cold and distant. There was a rough, cruel edge to her voice. There was a look on her face that was alien, completely unrecognisable from the woman I knew.

"Shitty things, they are nothing but trouble. You waste nine months carrying them, feeling ill, ruining your body. Then you spend god knows how many years feeding them, wiping their arses and pandering to their every need. All the time life passes you by. Its not right."

I was shocked by her words. She had never used such crude terms before. In fact she had chastised Angela for calling Tom a little shit when he was being particularly annoying. I remembered the confused look on Tom's face. Why was his sister calling him poo?

"But they are your life. Our children are our life. We wanted them. You wanted them. What has bought this on?"

“I've had enough of sacrificing my life to others. I don't exist, I am just a child minder. To you I am just a damn housekeeper. I am fed up with it. It's all wrong. I hate it.”

In the pause whilst I tried to let her outburst sink in Jane wondered off. We were no longer talking. She was simply blurting out whatever was in her head without reason or compassion. Who was this woman? I had tried to confront her but had achieved a worsening of the situation. She felt able to speak her innermost and darkest thoughts without constraint. I was not allowed the courtesy of a reply.

Later that evening I was scanning through the Web looking for something, anything that would give me some clue as to Jane's condition. I had always believed that nothing is unique. There are billions of people on the planet. Surely something like this had happened before? There was a lot of material about brain damage following illness but much of it was confused and from people who seemed to be little better than hypochondriacs. Expert testimony was scarce and general opinion seemed to be to seek medical advice from a doctor. As we had already done this the advice was pointless.

Rather than helping, my research only deepened my confusion. There was so much about the human condition we did not understand. The answer could not be found in the ether and the hundreds of rambling conversations of troubled people.

My thoughts were interrupted when I heard Tom clomping down the stairs in my shoes. Of course he had shoes of his own but somehow mine were more interesting. It was an innocent thing to do but I had tried to stop him walking downstairs wearing them. He offered considerable resistance so for the sake of peace I had conceded, However after some stern negotiation I had persuaded him to agree to hold on to the stair rails in case he tripped.

Slowly the clomping came nearer until finally Tom entered the room.

"Daddy, why is mummy staring at the wall?"

I looked up from the computer to see the strange sight of a small boy wearing shoes far too big for him and carrying a much abused toy rabbit. That pesky rabbit had been a constant source of trouble. He was forever losing it and was inconsolable until we found it again. What he did not know was that he was holding the third version of the rabbit. We had managed somehow to con him into thinking each replacement was the original.

Twice I had enacted the ridiculous ritual of battering a brand new cuddly toy and covering it with dirt and stains. I had become an expert at aging cuddly toys. But Tom was four years old now, and I held out the hope that perhaps he would soon lose interest and move on to something else. It was also unlikely I would be able to con him for a fourth time should he mislay the pesky thing again. He was getting far too worldly-wise. But this same maturity should see him become less rigidly attached to things. I had already resolved that there would not be a fourth version. If this one got lost he would have to face reality. It was part of growing up.

"What do you mean Tom?"

"She is sitting on the bed staring at something."

Immediately concerned that Jane had taken a turn for the worse I stood up and raced upstairs. Our doctor had warned us that we never completely get rid of viruses. The body copes with them and gets them under control but they remain lurking inside us. Sometimes these virulent viruses came back and we needed to watch for the signs. Was Jane experiencing another attack? The thought horrified me. What further damage might another attack do to her fragile brain?

Entering her bedroom I saw Jane sitting with the curtains drawn closed staring blankly in front of her. I had never seen such an expressionless face. Her facial muscles were completely relaxed. To all appearances the blood had drained from them.

"Are you alright Jane?"

Jane continued to stare blankly. Her breathing was shallow but regular as if practising some of the yoga on which she used to be so keen. I consoled myself that this was indeed what she was doing but the thought carried little conviction. In the past when I had interrupted such exercises I had received a withering look for disturbing her. Now there was nothing, not even a hint of recognition that I was there. But she looked calm and did not appear to be hot so I decided to leave her for a while.

Tom had clomped his way back upstairs following me and now stood behind me. Placing a reassuring hand on his head I ushered him out of the room.

"Come on, Mummy is doing some yoga. We must not disturb her."

"OK."

With a chirpy acceptance Tom clomped out of the room. How was I going to break him of this fascination with my shoes?

For the next three hours I looked in occasionally on Jane as she continued to sit motionless. I debated as to whether to call the doctor. What could I tell him? Jane was sitting peacefully and calm. They were hardly symptoms for concern.

When I looked in on her for the fourth time she was more awake and fidgeting slightly. Without looking at me she spoke in a calm but unfamiliar voice.

"Who is that man?"

I responded typically to a question heard but not understood. Asking someone to repeat the same question does not make it any clearer but buys some time to think. I needed to latch on to any chance to talk with this increasingly uncommunicative woman.

"Pardon?"

Mechanically Jane repeated the question in the same unfamiliar voice. This time she added the merest hint of a nod in the direction of the wall opposite.

"Who is that man?"

I looked at the area of the wall Jane was staring at. Was she hallucinating? Was this enough reason to call the doctor? In an instant she changed from her near lifeless state to one of more activity. She shook her head and picked up a book that lay on the bed beside her. It was as if a switch had been thrown and she had come to life.

"It's OK. He's gone now. When are you going to do something about that child's fetish with your shoes? I was trying to relax and all I could hear was that damn clomping."

There it was again, talking about the children as if they belonged to someone else not her. I heard myself trying to reason with her but she was paying little attention.

"Fetish is a bit strong. He is only playing. Its harmless. He will grow out of it in his own time."

Jane snorted with contempt.

"In the meantime the rest of us have to put up with it. If he really wants to fill your shoes he is going to have to grow up."

I did not want to continue this attack on Tom's innocent behaviour. Annoying it may be but it was harmless. We had come to an arrangement. He could wear my shoes so long as he was careful and I would wait for him to grow tired of them. But Jane talking about Tom in this way was an unwelcome distraction. I needed to understand what had just happened and indeed what had happened for the past few hours.

"Who was the man you were talking about?"

"What man?"

She looked at me puzzled. Her response seemed to be genuine innocence.

"Just now you asked me who that man was. There is no man in here, apart from me. Did you see someone. Were you dreaming?"

Jane was now scowling with annoyance.

"You are not making sense. If you have nothing sensible to say go away."

I was looking at a face I could barely recognise. Her features were set hard and her eyes dark and distant. There was no point carrying on with this conversation. Jane was in her own world and resented my presence. I decided that since she was awake and not apparently unwell I would leave her to her thoughts. I took away the challenge of how I could communicate with this increasingly isolated woman. She seemed to be occupying her own world, a world from which I was excluded. In an irrational moment I wondered whether she could be dangerous.

~ 5 ~

We were slowly coming to terms with 'weird mummy'. I had tried to persuade Tom to stop calling her that but gave up. I had to confess it was an accurate description. At least he was not being affected by her aggressive behaviour.

Though her behaviour was odd and unpredictable it did not disrupt our daily routine. The only significant change was that I had now assumed all domestic duties. This included driving the children to school a task Jane used to perform. Allied to the stress of work these additional duties were taking a toll on my health. However, I had no choice but to get on with it for the sake of the children.

Things took a turn for the worse in a worrying way. Our domestic routine was disturbed when Jane had started to wander off on her own. Without warning she would stand up and walk out of the house. Though her behaviour was strange what struck me as most odd was that until now she had shown no interest in the outside world. I had made several attempts to persuade her to go for a walk but they had all been forcefully rejected. Now without my prompting she was going out on her own. I took this as a good sign though was deeply uncomfortable with the unpredictable nature of it.

I first became aware of this strange development when sitting in the bedroom working. Tom and Angela came running up the stairs. They knew better than to disturb me when I was working so the urgency meant something was wrong. They had learned not to get their heads bitten off by the angry bear when he was working. Angela took several gasping breaths before speaking.

"Mummy has gone out."

"Gone out where?"

"I don't know. She just went out."

"Did she say anything?"

Angela's face assumed a pained expression and she looked down to the floor. I recognise the gesture. I had been trained in reading body language as part of my contract negotiating skills. Was she trying to hide something?

"No."

Tom looked at her and shook his head emphatically in disagreement. Unable to control his excitement he chastised his sister.

"Yes she did. She said we were a bloody nuisance. I remember. Bloody nuisance she said. That's not nice is it daddy?"

My confused instincts dictated my next question. I automatically assumed the wrong thing. Despite my increasingly intimate knowledge of Jane's wayward behaviour, it had to be the children's fault.

"What have you been doing?"

Angela looked up at me, her face a picture of innocence. Slowly it turned to disappointment that I could think her guilty of misbehaving. Sulking she looked to the ground again avoiding my eyes.

"Nothing."

I looked suspiciously at Tom who gazed back bemused.

"And what about you young man. What have you been doing?"

Protesting loudly Angela sprang to her brother's defence.

"He did not do anything. She just stood up and went out. She just...just...told us she was fed up with us and needed some peace."

"Fed up?"

Tom fidgeted impatiently and spoke excitedly.

"No, she said we were a bloody nuisance."

I was suddenly struck by panic. In the months we had been back Jane had never been out on her own. Why would she do that when she shrunk from everything that seemed new to her? She had not recognised us. She had not recognised her home. How would she cope with the chaos that lay outside? If she was effectively seeing things for the first time how would she react? My panic drove me to action and I barked at the kids.

"OK you two put your shoes on and we will go and look for her."

Fortunately the weather was mild so we were not delayed by the usual wrestling that formed the tortuous action of putting their coats on. How they constantly made such a simple exercise so complicated was beyond me. They had two arms and the coats had two sleeves. What could be simpler? Even a child could do it though not apparently my children. But I was spared that frustration today. They somehow managed to associate the right feet in the right shoes.

About fifty yards away from our house was a public park. It seemed a sensible place to head for since Jane had spent many hours there with the children. A popular place it boasted a child safe play area with a soft surface. There was also a coffee shop next to it. This rendered it a great attraction especially to mothers who could sit drink coffee and chat whilst their children played in the safe area.

It was a great favourite with our children as they were able to run free without my constant warning them to be careful not to damage or break anything. I was proud of our garden and my diligent efforts to maintain it. I did not take too kindly to them destroying my work. The restraint they were obliged to exercise in the back garden was not necessary in the park. If they damaged the plants there I could simply apologise to any nearby gardener and ignore the look of disapproval. It was my taxes that paid for the upkeep of the park so I felt a vague sense of righteousness. In more honest moments I had to admit I was displaying typical twenty first century hypocrisy of double standards.

Entering the park gates we soon found Jane sitting on a bench staring into the distance. Approaching cautiously I sat down beside her.

"Jane? Are you alright?"

Slowly she turned her head to look at me. A look of disappointment crossed her face. She was clearly not glad to see me. I looked at Angela and Tom who were studying Jane intently. Perhaps she would be glad to see them.

"We were worried about you."

Without interrupting her gaze Jane spoke in a voice full of chastisement. It was more irritation than re-assurance.

"There is no need."

Continuing to stare into the distance Jane pulled an odd face as if she were tasting something unpleasant.

"Have you noticed how people smell? Take that man coming towards us he smells of deceit. There is something in his life about which he is lying."

I looked around to see who she meant. Without moving her head or changing her look Jane had noticed a man coming along the path beside the bench. It was remarkable peripheral vision, or were her senses heightened? Had the damage to her brain enhanced her sense of sound and smell?

"I don't understand. How can someone smell of deceit?"

"Just like you smell of the ridiculous and those children smell of irritation. Everyone smells."

Her remark shocked me and I was lost for words. As the stranger walked past us Jane sniffed loudly.

"There you are. What did I tell you? Deceit. It's awful. He's a disgrace."

Turning his head sharply the stranger cast Jane an angry look and then glared at me. He snared at me in a hostile voice.

"What's her problem? What did she say?"

I held my hand up as a gesture of restraint.

"Nothing. She was talking about the problem we are having at home with our drains."

I waited and cringed inwardly. Surely he would not believe such a ridiculous story? In a perfect gesture of unintended irony the man sniffed loudly and walked on.

Seemingly oblivious to the problem she had caused Jane's attention had wandered elsewhere.

"If you are all here who is looking after him?"

"I'm not sure what you mean. Looking after who?"

"The man."

This was a worrying turn of events. Was Jane hallucinating? I knew the house to be empty. Uncertain as to what to do I decided the best course of action was to play along with her. I did not want to risk her fragile temper in such a public place by contradicting her.

"Perhaps we should go back and see if he's alright."

Jane looked fiercely at me. It was a look I had never seen before in all our years together. It was full of anger and much more I could not interpret.

"He won't want to see you! He hates your smell. Its too clean and juvenile."

She was making less and less sense. I grasped her arm gently pulling her to her feet.

"I will take that risk. Come on kids let's get Mummy home."

All this time Angela and Tom had stood transfixed, fascinated by Jane's behaviour. They had been unusually quiet for them but now exploded into life again. Tom pleaded with me with his most appealing voice. With the selfishness of youth he was thinking only of himself.

"Oh, can't we stay and play for a while? I'll be good, honest."

Angela laughed and took hold of Jane's other arm.

"Come on Tom. You couldn't be good if you tried."

Jane turned to Tom and gave him a wild stare.

"No, he's a bloody nuisance."

Tom comically placed his hands on his hips mimicking a habit of mine when exasperated. Rather than feeling chastised he was triumphant

"I told you she said we were a bloody nuisance."

"Alright Tom. That's enough. I have told you about using bad language."

"But weird mummy..."

"It does not matter what Mummy said. You must not use bad language. I want no more argument from you. And do not call her weird Mummy."

"But she is weird."

"Enough!"

Tom was upset, he hated being reprimanded by me. It happened rarely since even at his tender age we managed to come to an agreement on things through negotiation. I did not play the heavy handed father. I saw resorting to this as a failure on my part. But such control was difficult when under stress as now.

I turned my attention back to Jane. Once again she cast her eyes at Tom menacingly and smiled. What was going on inside her head? Had she relished Tom's upset? With the closeness of a loving relationship we start to know almost instinctively what someone else is thinking. At that moment I had no idea what Jane was thinking. It was a painful revelation. There was now a vast gulf between us.

As we all walked back Jane was silent except for occasionally sniffing and scowling with disapproval. Angela looked at me with concern but I had no answers for her. Tom was sulking and being dragged along reluctantly. I knew he would soon get over it. Something else would grab his attention. My chastisement would be forgotten.

Jane wandered off several times again. Something in the park seemed to be drawing her. We would find her sitting staring into the distance as if in a trance. I wanted to know what strange thoughts were going through her mind but she evaded all my questions. She would simply look at me and sniff. It would seem she did not like my smell.

It could not go on so the fourth time I decided I needed to confront her. Sitting next to her on the bench I held her hand and spoke quietly.

"Jane you cannot keep wandering off on your own like this."

She cast me a puzzled look.

"I can."

"Yes I know you can, what I mean is you must not. What if something happens to you?"

"Why do you care?"

"That is not fair. We care, me and the children."

Jane looked at me coldly and squinted half closing her eyes. What was she looking at? Was she trying to judge if I was sincere?

"I don't understand."

"Don't understand what?"

"Why am I here? "

"Why are you here in the park? Because you keep wandering off."

"No, what am I doing here? You tell me you are my husband and that those awful children are mine but it makes no sense."

It was another of those moments when what I was hearing was incomprehensible. How was I to respond to such nonsense? As we sat in silence for several minutes lost in our own thoughts I wondered whose thoughts were darkest. She suddenly sat upright and raised her voice.

"Someone is following me."

I was startled and looked around. There was no one.

"Who is following you?"

"A woman, she is looking for her children. And...."

She fell silent again and slumped back onto the bench. I was desperate to know exactly what she was thinking.

"And who? Do you mean there are two people following you?"

"I don't want to talk about it. He would not like it."

"Who would not like it?"

Jane sat staring ahead into the distance. Since she was making it clear this was the end of the conversation I held her arm and coaxed her off the bench. As we walked back slowly the silence continued. Though I was deeply concerned about her state of mind I was beginning to gain some understanding. The woman looking for her children could be Jane or rather the old Jane. But this man was a mystery. It was the second time she had mentioned him. Whoever he was she was scared of him.

After a great deal of arguing I managed to persuade Jane not to wander off on her own. She reacted badly to my prompting but I was firm. There was still the danger she could have a relapse. Worse case she could pass out and need help. Who helps strangers in this day and age? And then there was the strange sniffing. I had already seen how a stranger could react to it.

I was not convinced my entreaties were the reason Jane ceased to wander. I got the impression she had been looking for something and had either found it or given up the search. It was impossible to tell what was going on in her troubled mind.

Jane had reverted back to her fear of going outside. I had asked the kids to keep a very close eye on her and warn me of the first sign she was about to wander off again but after a week they had stopped their constant watching. Jane showed no sign of wanting to venture out.

Jane seemed content to stay in and spend hours on the computer. It was slightly odd since previously she had avoided using one as much as possible. I also had concerns about the isolated nature of using a computer when I wanted her to communicate. But I was at a complete loss as to what to do and decided to let sleeping dogs lie. Locked into the computer the strange bad tempered woman left us in peace.

~ 6 ~

It was a little after three o'clock in the morning when I was awoken by some odd noises coming from downstairs. I listened for a while trying to determine what or who it was. It was unlikely to be Angela. Once she was asleep she slept for nine or ten hours and nothing woke her. I often had to shake her quite hard to get up in the morning. I had been assured this was normal for a child of her age. Growing was tiring.

From the noise it was more likely to be Tom. He could not do anything quietly. But it sounded too methodical and deliberate to be Tom. He did everything erratically. His mind tended to wander from whatever task he was supposed to be doing and the lack of concentration resulted in chaos. A process of elimination therefore brought me to conclude that it was Jane.

I sat up quickly at the realisation. What was she doing in the middle of the night? I walked slowly and quietly downstairs. As a child I had been prone to sleep walking. I would walk downstairs and my parents would find me busy doing something but completely asleep. Given Jane's fragile state could this be what she was doing? If so my own experience told me that I had to be careful. Waking someone from such a sleep can be dangerous. I always thought it strange that it was considered more dangerous to wake someone than them walking downstairs asleep. But despite my unconscious night time wandering I never came to harm.

In the kitchen I found Jane very much awake and scrubbing the kitchen sink with a frenzy.

"Jane, what are you doing? Is everything alright?"

Without stopping her feverish scrubbing she spoke harshly.

"You should not be in bed at this time. Did you know its the most likely time to have a heart attack?"

It was an odd remark. Her father Edward had died of a stroke in the middle of the night. Is this what she was remembering? If so it was a healthy sign if somewhat perverse. It was the first indication that her memory was returning. As I stood hesitating to reply I remembered the caution of the doctor. He told me to be careful with returning memories. They can come as a shock especially if the memory is of something unpleasant or traumatic. We handle many events emotionally and if we have lost or forgotten that emotion a memory can be difficult to cope with. It was important to encourage the memory but gently so as not to unleash the emotions associated with it.

"Are you thinking about Edward?"

"Edward who?"

"Your father."

Jane looked up from her labour and stared at me intensely. Her mind seemed to be racing frantically.

"My father?"

"Yes. He had a heart attack in the early hours of the morning."

Jane shrugged her shoulders without a hint of emotion and resumed her scrubbing. It was as if talk of the father she had loved so much was interfering with her work. Pausing she stared at the window opposite the sink her mind deep in thought.

"I was reading about it the other day. Statistics show the most likely time for a heart attack is three o'clock in the morning. So if you are not in bed at that time you reduce the risk."

She resumed her industry with vigour. My apparently healthy heart sank with disappointment. This was not a memory but another punctuated rambling. I had noticed that often when she spoke there seemed to be no connection with what was going on around her. It was as if she were sharing an alternate private world with us. It would appear that this cleaning activity was springing from that strange personal world in which she dwelt. She was seeing an unclean world that needed her attention.

As she scrubbed Jane sniffed loudly. She still seemed to be smelling things that offended her. After each sniff she would attack the offending spot.

"Why are you cleaning?"

"Its the bacteria. I read that it can get into your blood and damage your heart valves. You must keep this place cleaner. Those kids make a terrible mess. Kids are breeding grounds for bugs. They pass them around each other and we have to face the consequences. It would be much safer if they weren't around."

As I stood watching, lost for words, I guessed that she had been studying something on the Internet. I began to realise that her behaviour was child like. She had learnt a new fact, absorbed it and acted on it as if it was a universal truth of profound significance. It was just like a young child. When it learns something new it possesses it almost obsessively. I had seen this behaviour in both Angela and Tom.

"You are as strong as an ox Jane. You have nothing to worry about."

Jane looked up with a puzzled expression on her face.

"But I have been very ill. He told me."

"The doctor? Yes, he was very worried about you. We all were. But you are better now."

"Better than what?"

"Better than when you were ill."

"This conversation is not making sense. I didn't mean the doctor. He was useless."

She was right, the conversation had lost me. If not the doctor the who had told her she was ill?

"So who did you mean?"

"No one you know."

Sniffing once more Jane seemed satisfied with the sink and moved on to the work top. It looked clean to me. I had washed it earlier after finishing our meal. But it would appear it was not clean enough for Jane. Though I was struggling with the conversation Jane was talking to me. It was a rare occurrence I wanted to exploit.

"What other things should we be careful about?"

"Lots. Life is very fragile. You are here one minute and gone the next. Did you know that until recently the most likely age to die was zero?"

"I don't follow."

"The most likely time to die was in your first year of birth."

"You say 'was' does that mean it has changed?"

"Yes. Its sixty something now. And you are most likely to die of a heart attack. The most likely time to die was before your first birthday, but the most likely cause is a heart attack which a baby does not suffer. That's very strange isn't it?"

"So what you are saying..."

I was not allowed to reply. It was a rhetorical question. As was her custom Jane was talking to me not with me.

"So that is the next target. To increase the most likely age to die from sixty. That's why we must not be asleep at three and must get rid of all these germs. Then we can increase the age to seventy or more. And once the most likely time to die is seventy that means an awful lot more people will live way beyond it."

Suddenly Jane dropped the cloth she was holding took a deep breath and sighed. Staggering two steps backwards she slumped onto a chair.

"I'm tired. Its hard work all this cleaning. You should get someone in to do it. Or perhaps those messy children could do it."

As I watched anxiously I saw Jane's eyes flicker as she fought to stay awake. I walked over and gently grabbed her arm.

"Come on. Let's get you back to bed. I will finish off down here."

Through half closed eyes Jane looked up at me.

"You will? Good. He will be pleased."

"Who will be pleased?"

I desperately wanted to know who she was talking about but her eyes started to close so I made haste to lead her back upstairs.

Throughout the following day I pondered on the events of the night. It would seem that Jane's mind could easily be disturbed and by the oddest things. If indeed she were learning life from new again I needed to be very cautious. I was not sure how but I would have to monitor what she was reading and what she did. Simply throwing things at a blank canvas could be harmful. There was much on the Internet that could harm a fragile mind.

I paid particular attention to cleaning ensuring Jane was fully aware of my endeavours. I did it with a flourish and a lot of noise, much to the amusement of the children. Tom in particular took great pleasure in mimicking me complete with heavy breathing and grunting. I was unsure as to whether pandering to this apparent obsession was the right thing to do but I was making it up as I went along. Having to deal with someone as fragile as Jane was new to me. She had always been so strong and resourceful. All my energies had been applied to the children. I had never needed to worry about Jane. In fact she rejected any fuss.

Whatever the rights or wrongs of my behaviour it seemed to work. Jane did not get up in the night again except for the occasional bathroom visit. There was a suspicion that the motor senses of her brain had been mildly affected and that perhaps her bladder control could have been weakened. My own suspicion is that bad dreams were disturbing her and driving her out of bed. Perhaps a visit to the toilet reset the bad dreams,

Certainly there were odd signs of her inability to control muscle movements but nothing serious. She would motion to walk but there would be a slight delay before her legs moved. It was as if her brain was saying move but her legs were resisting. I tried not to find amusement in the puzzled look on her face as her legs disobeyed her. I was horrified to see one day Tom copying his mothers awkward movement. After a long and stern negotiation I persuaded him not to repeat it. It lingered long in my mind that Tom was making fun of his mother. Had all emotional contact between them gone? Had he lost his mother? How would this affect his development? There was so much uncertainty about our future.

~ 7 ~

Our life was ticking by but it was erratic and uncertain. At any time Jane could do something unusual or bizarre and completely disrupt the rhythm. I felt compelled to do something to re-establish normality. Perhaps I was deluding myself such a thing was possible but I had to try. I was beginning to feel I was a stranger in a world that was not mine. I longed for the family we were just a few months ago. That comfortable life was a fading memory I wanted to resurrect. But whatever I tried it always seemed just out of reach.

Perhaps we needed to do something as a family. I decided on a shopping trip, something Jane should enjoy and we could all do together. Would this take her out of the strange world into which she seemed to have withdrawn? I could but try.

Some time during the late twentieth century someone had come up with the expression retail therapy. Perhaps it was from the mind of some clever but cynical marketing person. It reflected the mentality of the age. In Jane's case shopping represented a break from the everyday things of life. She enjoyed the occasional outing but was not a spendthrift. She only bought what was actually necessary but took pleasure in the activity. My hope was that a trip would indeed act as some form of therapy. Equally significantly it was one of the few things we did together as a family. All objections by the children were dismissed. Once we were in the shops they revelled in the activity.

In common with most modern families mealtimes had become a chaotic activity and it was rare that we all sat down together. Even Sundays were manic as the kids were usually rushing out somewhere. Or rather, we were rushing them out as unpaid taxi drivers. Shopping was a common activity everyone looked forward to. My own loathing of the tiresome activity was suppressed for the sake of harmony. I contented myself with the knowledge that it was something they wanted to do. I was not flushed with altruism or a martyr but rather I appreciated the comparative peace a shopping trip bought.

We were in a large department store with an extensive collection of clothing. Angela had recently put on a growth spurt and needed some larger clothes. She was also experiencing some peer pressure at school. Some of her friends were wearing clothes from some fashion trend. Though we refused to subscribe to trends for overly priced designer clothes there was a certain way we were prepared to go. Children can be cruel and we wanted to protect her as best we could. It was a juggling act between buying her clothes that were acceptable in her circle of friends but not pandering to ridiculous fashion. I wanted her to be strong. She had to learn to cope with how others behaved. She needed to learn to be independent and stand up for herself.

I knew that as parents we were not alone in wrestling with this problem. Weak parents tended to give in whilst the stronger made a stand. We tended to try to meet the children's demands half way. The problem was that the half way point was tricky to determine. To my mind it was defined by just how much we could get away with without too much protest from the children. But it was a movable point often shifted by tears.

Jane and Angela were browsing through racks of young girls clothes as Tom and I stood by watching. They appeared not to be able to agree. In fact they were disagreeing about every item of clothing. A halfway meeting point appeared to be a long way off. I was losing patience but struggling manfully to retain it. At least externally I appeared to be retaining my patience. Tom had most definitely lost his and was becoming petulant and surly.

Bored children find things to amuse themselves. Unfortunately these things tend to be naughty. Its as if they are protesting against the boredom. Shopping for girls clothes was of no interest to Tom and he was on the verge of becoming a nuisance and misbehaving. We were on the ground floor of the department store and since it was women's clothing there was nothing to distract him. I let Jane and Angela walk off to another rack of clothes while I got to grips with the restless boy.

Several minutes later as I tried to distract the restless Tom an odd but somehow familiar noise caught my attention. Across the expansive shop floor I could see Angela crying. I was familiar with her naughty child cry and her cry of pain but this was different. It was a cry of the deepest distress; crying I had never heard before. It was a cry that cut deep into my parental feelings appealing to my base instincts of protection. I grabbed Tom and rushed over.

As I approached I saw that a burly, slightly unkempt man was clutching Angela's right arm and confronting Jane.

"Is this your child madam?"

Jane shrugged her shoulders dismissing the question.

"Little brat is nothing to do with me."

To my horror, Jane turned and walked away across the shop floor. By now I had reached the man and I confronted him with as much ferocity as I could conjure for the normally passive person I was.

"Take your hands off my daughter or I will have you arrested for assault."

"I have observed this child take something from a shelf and put it in her bag."

I was incensed and angry and shouted as loudly as I could.

"Don't be stupid, my daughter is not a thief you idiot."

"Shouting abuse at me will not help sir. I would like you both to come with me."

Slowly the man released his grip on my sobbing daughter. As I looked anxiously at Angela's continued distress I was confused. Blind instinct told me Angela was not a thief but common sense told me this man would not be making such an accusation without cause. This was a situation I had never experienced before and was struggling to cope with what seemed so unreal. In life we learn from experiences but a new experience needs time and careful contemplation. I had neither in the immediacy of the situation. I did not possess the instinct to react rationally. Meekly I grabbed Angela's hand and followed the man pulling the reluctant girl behind me. Her sobbing had subsided but she was still whimpering in distress.

We stood in a small room at the back of the store waiting for the next move from the unpleasant security guard. In his hand he held a bright pink bag which I recognised as Angela's. Opening the bag the man extracted a pale blue ladies blouse still in its clear plastic bag. He held it aloft triumphantly and waited for my reaction. Allowing time for the shock to pass I slowly I bent down to look at Angela face to face.

"Angela I need you to tell me why you picked this up and put it in your bag."

"Mummy told me to."

"You mean mummy asked you to pick up this blouse and put it in your bag?"

"Yes. She said it was a game."

"A game?"

"Yes. She said if I did it properly I would get a reward. But I had to do it without being seen."

By now I had started to collect myself again and was getting annoyed with the almost smug look on the store detective's face. He was taking an unhealthy and perverse pleasure in the situation. I longed to erase the 'told you so' look but sensibly reasoned that violence was not the answer. Besides I had heard about some of these security guards. They were barely tame thugs familiar with violence.

"Look, my daughter is clearly not a thief. She thought she was playing a game. Is there some way we can resolve this without resorting to anything too extreme?"

"There's a sign at the entrance. Its company policy to prosecute all shop lifters without exception. If we show any signs of weakness thieves will rob us blind."

Fortunately my mind was starting to become lucid and rational again. I needed to get control of the situation.

"As I understand it you have to prove that there was no intention to pay for the item?"

After first nodding with enthusiasm the guard started to hesitate. What little brain he had was working hard.

"Er, yes. Your wife has left the store so she had no intention of paying."

"But my daughter, myself and the item are still in the store. I am offering you payment now. There has been no actual theft and no intention of leaving without paying."

A ridiculous scowl crossed the man's face as he thought as deeply as his limited capacity would allow. With a slow intake of breath and sharp sigh he admitted defeat.

"OK sir. Technically you are correct so perhaps we will overlook this indiscretion this time."

I felt small twinge of triumph and a lot of anger.

"This time? There is no this time. Nothing has happened. There will not be a next time."

With considerable hostility the man folded him arms and raised his voice.

"There most certainly will not. None of your family are welcome in this store, so do not come back."

With a pointless wave of his arm the man dismissed us. As I stood watching the unpleasant man walk back into the store I looked down at Angela. She seemed much calmer almost as if the events of the past few minutes had never happened. How quickly children move on. Its only as adults that we tend to dwell on things and let the full impact hit us. Life for children is far more immediate. Life is an adventure, something happens and they move on to the next thing. It does not dwell nagging them.

For me however life could not move on. I needed to understand what was happening. I paid for the blouse as quickly as possible and left the store with the children clasping my hands on either side. It was a futile, almost comical act of defiance and unity. Tom was still being difficult but I tugged him with a force I had never used before. Such unusual aggression calmed him down though the precedent sat uncomfortably with me. Normally I would negotiate with the kids and be defiant in the battle of wills. I did not bully my children but the extreme circumstance was bringing out the worst in me.

Opening the front door to our house I heard the sound of the vacuum cleaner. This was a surprise. Apart from the strange incident in the kitchen Jane had not done any sort of cleaning in the four months we had been home. As I walked into the front room followed by the children Jane looked up.

"This house is a mess. Your kids need to be a lot tidier."

I was dumbstruck. Jane was acting as if nothing had happened. She was also absolving herself of all responsibility for the children. They were mine not hers.

I was determined she could not just ignore what had taken place but I could not confront her in front of the children. I ushered them both upstairs to their rooms. As Tom started to object I gave him a fierce look and he understood immediately. He had after all seen a rougher side of Daddy as I had tugged him forcefully out of the store. As the kids walked upstairs I went over to the cleaner and pressed my foot on the off button.

"Is it true you told Angela to take that blouse?"

Jane waved a casual hand as if to dismiss the ridiculous question.

"I can't be held responsible for the way your child behaves. Perhaps you should have bought her up properly."

My mind could not understand the detached way she spoke about our daughter. Angela was our child not just my child.

"What do you mean, my child? She is your child too."

Jane made no reply. It was as if a shutter had gone up. This was a characteristic of her behaviour that was becoming increasingly familiar. When faced with a reality she did not want to acknowledge she simply closed into herself. She refused to engage in conversation and her face adopted the hard and detached appearance that was becoming so familiar. To all intents and purposes I did not exist.

At that moment in time I felt alone. I was losing the children and the woman I had known was still somewhere else. I was feeling powerless in the face of an onslaught to our lives. How could a simple shopping trip have ended so badly? It was supposed to have bought us together as a family not driven us further apart. I needed to be guarded and thoughtful about everything I did from now on. Even the simple things could go horribly wrong with this strange woman. Worse, she was capable of dragging the children with her. She could exploit their naivety.

~ 8 ~

I had arrived home from work tired and angry. These worrying developments at home had made me intolerant of office politics. Until recently the back stabbing and conspiracies washed over me and I stayed calm and aloof from them. I cared little for the ambitions of others. If they wanted to stamp all over people it was not my problem. But they would not stamp on me. Work place bullies soon back down if they realise you stand up to them. Stand firm, maintain your integrity and the harm they can do is limited.

My job was a means to an end and in my current difficult situation was an annoying but necessary inconvenience. The money was good but it was not a part of my life I took any pleasure in. I never allowed what happened in my job to reflect on the family. Parked on the driveway I would sit in the car prior to entering the house counting to ten, one hundred, one thousand, or however many it took to calm down and get myself into a more relaxed frame of mind. I had to be sure that I had left work behind and would not take out the stress on my family.

It was an odd but necessary ritual which both children had learnt never to interrupt. They knew they needed to let the angry bear calm down. Sometimes I would see Tom's face at the window watching me. He would be eagerly waiting to greet me with whatever excitement had filled his day but had learnt to wait until I had got rid of my demons. Angry bear Daddy was not nice especially since Tom would certain to be in some sort of trouble. He attracted it remorselessly. He was always keen to tell his side of the story first before Jane had chance. What his explanations lack in clarity they made up for in enthusiasm.

As I opened the front door and walked into the hallway I heard raised voices. Jane was shouting and Angela was making an odd noise which I could only describe as a cross between frustration and pleading. Entering the kitchen I saw Jane raise her hand above her head and land a heavy blow on the side of Angela's face sending her staggering backwards. Stumbling Angela fell to the floor banging her head on a chair. As I rushed towards Angela's semi-conscious body Jane turned and left the room. To my horror I noticed a calm smile cross her face. Had she taken pleasure in the assault? It was an unthinkable notion I dismissed immediately but it stayed lurking in the back of my mind as I examined Angela.

As I gently raised the sobbing girl I noticed a trickle of blood running from the side of her face. Though the wound seemed minor it was on a part of her forehead that bled profusely. Grabbing a towel hanging nearby I gently dabbed the wound to wipe away the blood. As I consoled Angela I remembered reading that head injuries to children could be serious since their skulls were not as developed as an adults. Should I take her to hospital?

Though Angela was growing fast I still had the strength to pick up her slight frame. Gently I carried her into the lounge where Jane was sat watching television as if nothing had happened. I lay Angela down on the sofa and stood in front of the screen and confronted her.

"What were you thinking Jane? How could you hit her like that?"

In vain Jane tried to look round me at the screen.

"You're in the way."

I moved even further to block her view. Exasperated I angrily raised my voice.

"Answer me!"

"She deserved it. She's been a bloody nuisance all day."

It was clear there was no reasoning with her and my concern for Angela was more pressing.

"We are going to take Angela to the hospital to have her head wound checked."

I was shocked to find myself grabbing Jane by the arm and forcefully pulling her to her feet.

"Get up, you are coming with me. This is your responsibility and you will face up to it."

As she stood it was unclear whether Jane was being submissive or simply could not be bothered to put up any resistance. My anger certainly gave me strength she would have found difficult to resist. Either way she came easily and without complaint. There was a strange distance in her eyes as if she were in a trance. Her behaviour was deeply worrying.

As usual the casualty department at our local hospital was in a chaotic state. I was sure there must have been some order to what went on but it was not apparent as we queued patiently waiting to register with the receptionist. Patients and staff were moving around in a manner similar to a nest of ants. As they hurried to and fro they managed to avoid bumping into each other. Occasionally they acknowledged each other but then moved swiftly on. I am sure their scurrying was important but it looked unnecessary to my uninformed eye. It was such a waste of energy.

We did not have long to wait. In these places children took priority and were always seen as soon as possible. A sympathetic nurse made a cursory examination of Angela's head and beckoned us to follow.

In a cubicle defined only by some curtains made slightly ragged by excessive washing and pulling back we were seen by another nurse who specialised in children. She certainly seemed to have a way with children as her friendly banter bought Angela out of herself and got her to start talking again. In my near panic and confusion I had not noticed that Angela was in a state of mild shock. The trauma of what had happened had affected her badly and she had not spoken a word since the incident. The only outward signs that she was conscious of what was around her were the occasional glances at Jane. It was nothing more than a flick of her eyes but they were eyes filled with fright. I had strived so hard to protect our children. I had never imagined that they were in danger in their own home.

As I sat on a chair on the opposite side of the treatment couch Jane stood in the corner watching what was going on. She had adopted that awful detached look again as if this was nothing to do with her. Was her twisted mind somehow managing to blame me? Or was it my mind that was becoming twisted with confusion and seeing the worst?

Several times the nurse looked round at Jane and gave her a quizzical look. I tried desperately to redress the balance by smiling with such exaggeration it must have looked comical; or perhaps it just looked weird. My ridiculous thoughts were interrupted by the triumphant sound of the nurses voice.

“There you go. All done. You'll have a nice pretty bruise as a trophy to show your friends. Its nothing serious Mister Cotter: just a little bump and flesh wound. Can you just wait here a minute and we will sort out the paperwork.”

As I watched her go my mind was still churning. Did she walk away with more speed than necessary or was she simply that type of person: all haste and urgency? Perhaps there was a queue of other patients needing her attention. What paperwork was she talking about?

My thoughts were interrupted as Angela touched her forehead and winced.

“What does it look like Daddy?”

I tried to smile as reassuringly as I could.

“You can hardly see anything. You're still very pretty.”

Angela's eyes again flicked in the direction of Jane who looked away avoiding contact. I was still in a state of confusion unsure as to what I should do about what had happened. If Jane was becoming violent then I could not ignore it. I held Angela's hand in truth more to comfort myself than her. In times of uncertainty it is a comfort to feel something tangible. I hoped it worked for both of us.

There was a flurry of movement in the ragged curtains and a woman walked in. She was middle aged and her clothing suggested she was not either a nurse or doctor but someone more official. There was a definite air of formality about her manner. Perhaps she processed the paperwork the nurse mentioned.

"Mister Cotter? I wonder if I could have a word with you."

Still confused from what had happened I found myself asking a ridiculous question.

"It is about Angela?"

I mentally kicked myself. Of course it was about Angela. She would hardly want to talk to me about where I had parked the car. I needed to get a grip of myself. I had always prided myself on being calm in a crisis but this control seemed to be slipping. In practice my control was over things which did not matter unlike this which mattered a lot.

"Yes. I just need a few details. It won't take long."

Instinctively I looked back at Jane. Could I leave her with Angela? Surely nothing would happen with all these people around? In a reflection of what had happened the thought hit me like the blow in the face Angela had received. I was not trusting Jane to be alone with the children. Suddenly the thought of Tom struck me and I panicked. Where was he? I looked around frantically. My mind was struggling to juggle with everything that was going on and I had forgotten about Tom. I really was losing a grip on things.

As if reading my thoughts the woman spoke.

"One of my colleagues is looking after your little boy. They are playing in the children's room."

As rapidly as it came my panic passed and turned to relief.

"Thank you. He does tend to wander off and it can be a challenge keeping up with him."

A smile of recognition crossed the woman's face.

"I know what you mean. He does seem a lively little boy. What is he, four years old?"

"Yes, just over. Four and three months. You know how important the extra months are to children."

"I remember mine at that age, full of energy and curiosity. Its an impossible job trying to keep up with them. They're so curious about the world."

I frowned at the chatty woman. Why was I suspicious of the small talk? She was only being friendly. We had reached a small room at the back of the treatment area. It was shabby and full of a selection of bits and pieces that would be expected to be found in such an area such as old crutches and boxes of disposable gloves. It was not so much a store room as a dumping area. It was doubtful anyone took much care stashing things in the chaotic room.

We sat on two chairs facing each other whilst the woman took a note pad out of an ancient briefcase. Her friendly smile of a minute ago had turned to something more strict and less welcoming. Perhaps I had some cause to be suspicious.

"For my records could I ask precisely how this happened? "

"I have already explained to the doctor. She fell and hit her head on a chair. You know kids, always charging around. Why do you ask? Why are you interested? What is it you do here?"

"I am from the child welfare department. You must understand that with any accident to a child requiring hospital treatment we are obliged to watch for any signs of abuse."

"What?"

"You would be surprised at the number of children we get in here that have fallen over, or hit themselves on a door, or any number of apparently accidental mishaps. We are obliged to look into them. I have spoken with your wife. She seems a little detached. Most mothers would be upset when one of their children is injured. She seems, I don't know, not quite here. Is she on any medication?"

"Medication? No. Why do you ask?"

I felt uncomfortable repeating the same confused questions but I was buying time to think.

"There is something about the glazed look in her eyes. I see it in patients on some types of medication."

I found myself speaking an apology which sounded less than convincing. My confused state seemed to be generating reasonable responses to the questioning but I felt detached from them. Someone else seemed to be answering. It was as if someone other than me was talking about a stranger.

"Bringing up two small children is hard work. She is probably tired."

An awkward silence fell between us. In the passing seconds I began to suspect she was trying to work out how to say something difficult. She looked at me several times apparently trying to assess me. Was she trying to understand if I was a violent type?

"Were you aware that your daughter has bruises on her ribs?"

The underlying significance of the question escaped me. Both children always had little knocks and bruises and it was not unusual for us not to understand where they had come from. Most of the time the children could not remember how they got them. Indeed there were many occasions when they did not realise they had them. They would come to light when they were undressing or having a bath.

"She must have got them during the fall."

"No, the doctor believes they are several days old. He could tell from the colouring."

I racked my brain frantically for anything that had happened to Angela in the past few days.

"Your little boy, Tom, has he had any accidents recently?"

"Well, he did fall off....."

I stopped immediately. This conversation was starting to get ominous. The underlying significance of the questions now screamed at me. Actually both children had been accident prone recently; more accident prone than usual. I had accepted Jane's explanations without question. She was their mother and the woman I knew so well to be loving and caring. Why would I not believe her?

Again I heard my less than convincing voice.

"You know kids. They are always getting into scrapes and hurting themselves. We can't wrap them in cotton wool can we?"

Despite my concerned state my brain was still functioning. I was reverting to psychology to try to relate with my inquisitor. I was trying to appeal to her reasonableness.

Slowly she nodded in agreement but the gesture lacked conviction.

"Of course. I understand. I have mentioned that I have children of my own and they are always knocking themselves. It is part of growing up. I sometimes feel that a child is not normal unless they have a bruise or scrape."

Did her voice have a patronising edge or was I looking for problems? She continued with authority and assurance.

"I understand that your wife recently had a serious illness. I am going to recommend that someone visits regularly to check she is coping OK."

Looking into the fixed eyes of the woman I realised that this was not a negotiable suggestion. She was telling me what was going to happen. I also realised that this was almost certainly a smoke screen. What she was really suggesting was that they wanted to check on the children.

A darkness covered my thoughts. I felt little option but to submit without argument. If I could not accept a reasonable suggestion then possibly I too would be flagged as a potential problem. One parent under suspicion is bad enough but two would almost certainly trigger loud alarms. Who knows where it would lead? I had to be calm and reasonable. I repeated to myself that I had to get a grip. I needed to be a reasonable man. They had to see me as a reasonable caring father.

"If you think that a sensible precaution then by all means. Jane has been struggling a bit since her illness so I would appreciate some help."

"Good. I will get that organised. Coping with two young children is not easy if you are not feeling one hundred percent."

She was scribbling furiously on her note pad. At that moment it seemed a little odd to me that she was still using pen and paper when the world was moving onto electronic devices. Perhaps it was a matter of protecting personal data. Paper was so much easier to protect than digital information. I suddenly realised that in the middle of this mess I was thinking about work. Was it a bad sign that my mind was wandering? I tried to come back down to earth. Here was a woman probing my family and I had no idea who she was. What sort of power did she have? Should I be in fear of her? Child welfare seemed to be constantly in the news.

"I'm sorry, I don't know your name."

"That's not important. I am simply doing the preliminaries. We will assign someone more permanent to your case."

I was shocked to hear her use the word case. What did that mean? I was about to question her further when she looked me hard in the eyes.

"I am sure you want to get back to your daughter. They will have finished with her by now. Thank you for your time. We will be in touch soon."

I realised it was a polite but firm dismissal. If I had any questions or anything further to say it would not be countenanced. I left her scribbling notes on the substantial note pad. Clearly she was a copious note taker. I was struck with the lingering concern that our talk had been too brief. How could she make a valid assessment in such a short space of time? How could such a potentially damning and life changing judgement have been made so quickly? I knew these people were busy but they had the power to make life shattering decisions. Surely this warranted more time?

Jane and the children were sitting waiting for me in reception. An uncomfortable silence lay over them. Only Tom showed any sense of normality as he swung his legs beneath his chair and looked around him. He was a restless child. Though everything in life was a new adventure he soon became bored.

We drove back in silence. Jane seemed to be half asleep whilst Angela and Tom sat in the back flicking through some magazines and comics we had bought in the hospital shop. They weren't really reading. It was if they were trying to distract themselves from everything around them. This lack of communication made me feel isolated. There was so much we needed to discuss but no one was talking. This latest event was threatening to take a serious turn with unthinkable consequences. We were being suspected of abusing our children. Wasn't the father usually the prime suspect? Didn't they always side with the mother? Unrest was taking over my normally calm world.

~ 9 ~

It was an unpleasantly cold and wet day when we received the first visit from the welfare worker. When I opened the door she stood in the entrance looking bedraggled. From inside her ridiculously ample handbag she extracted an identity card and held it in front of my face.

"Mister Cotter? June Saunders."

I squinted at the card struggling to read it in the poor light. Why do they always laminate these cards? My heart sank at what I read and the implications the words carried. Though I had been expecting her I had harboured hope they would change their mind and she would not come. The news often carried stories about lack of resources. Surely there were more urgent cases than ours?

I beckoned her inside and offered to take her rain soaked coat. She smiled slightly uncomfortably as she struggled to remove the garment made heavy by the rain. It was reminiscent of the struggles Angela and Tom always had removing their coats. Perhaps they would never grow out of it. Miss Saunders had apparently not.

"Thanks. It's miserable out there isn't it? I do so detest this time of year. I have always said we should hibernate like some animals do and come out when its Spring again."

My heightened senses were working overtime. Was this small talk to play down the situation or simply a young woman being polite? Mentally I chastised myself. She was only doing her job. How could I rush to judge so quickly? I needed to give her time; everyone deserved that. I had failed to shake her hand. Would she see this as a black mark against me? I knew enough about psychology to know that physical contact was a sign of being open. I wanted to grab her hand but after the time that had elapsed it would have seemed strange. In fact it could almost have seemed like an assault. She had not proffered her hand. Perhaps physical contact was frowned upon in her line of work. Or possibly she had seen too many parents react angrily and kept her distance. My mind staggered from question to question as I tried to calm myself.

As I showed her into the front room where Jane and the kids were I determined that she would see a happy family playing together. She would be able to report that all was well and the children were in a loving relationship. As I introduced Jane she simply raised her eyes to look at Saunders. Her head remained stationary as did the rest of her body as she sat motionless. In response to the inquisitive look from Saunders I whispered quietly.

"She is not feeling too bright. I will explain later."

Saunders seemed satisfied so I gestured for her to sit down.

"Ah yes. The case notes mention your wife's illness. It sounds like it was very bad."

My mind rebelled at the mention of case notes. This is the expression the stern woman had used in casualty. It was cold and clinical. How could they use such an expression where living, breathing people were involved?

I needed to know what was on this woman's mind. I decided to ask a question I already knew the answer to.

"What is the purpose of your visit?"

"I just wanted to meet you and the children and see what help if any you needed."

Saunders flicked her eyes in Jane's direction. Jane was staring at the wall opposite in the distant manner that was becoming so familiar. She was physically present but her mind was elsewhere. I felt the desperate need to do something to show all was well.

I sat on the floor at the coffee table and played with the kids. It was one of those ridiculous games kids enjoy so much but seem so infantile to adults. But it was vaguely educational.

I needed to make the right impression. I knew the kids would rather be doing other things. Angela especially would rather be playing on her computer chatting to her friends. Tom would have preferred to be creating chaos in some form. But for now, there was no arguing, we were all going to play together. Despite their tender years the children had sensed this was important. They at least still listened to me and respected me. If I was to be inspected and interrogated by this woman she would do it while I played with the children.

My desperate plan was receiving a damaging blow. Jane continued to sit staring into space. She had told me she had a headache. She was given to these as a long term effect of the virus. However, I was increasingly suspicious that this was a convenient way for her to shut us and the world out. She seemed to be able to turn headaches on and off at will. She would sit motionless whilst we trod carefully and quietly so as not to disturb her. Perversely, I had learnt to enjoy these periods of comparative calm. Whilst disturbing a silent motionless Jane meant nothing strange was happening. But at this moment in time it was potentially damaging,

I felt anger welling up inside and my mind started to rage. We needed to put on a good show and Jane was being uncooperative. She was making things worse. What would this women think of such behaviour? Was it appropriate for a mother? It was her fault we were in this situation. She could make the effort to help make amends. How could she just shut everything out?

At least Angela and Tom were playing the game. The presence of Saunders was keeping them calm and well behaved and I was convinced she would be satisfied with such balanced children. My own behaviour was more difficult to assess. I probably looked on edge and worried especially with the way Jane was behaving. But if this woman was any good at her job surely she would understand?

After about thirty minutes of watching and chatting idly about nothing of significance it seemed that Saunders had seen enough. Pointedly she stood up and spoke quietly to me.

"Could you spare me a few minutes to answer some questions? Is there somewhere we can go?"

I looked at her with deep suspicion. Had she not seen enough? Had she not seen a contented family at play? Was she keen to get away from Jane and interrogate me about her?

"Questions? What sort of questions?"

"I just need to understand a little more about you and the family. Its just for the records. Nothing to worry about."

There it was again: just for the records, nothing to worry about. All these people used such expressions as if it bestowed harmlessness on their activities. I ushered her into the dining room next door and we sat at the table opposite each other.

"Your wife was very quiet, is she OK?"

"She is not quite herself. She has a headache."

"Does your wife often get headaches?"

Was this a trick question or a genuine inquiry? I was on guard and very wary about anything I said.

"I am not sure how often is often."

"Several times a week, once a day. More often than you get one."

"We were warned that they could be an effect of the virus. But they do not last. She sits quietly for a while and the go away. We are hoping they will clear up eventually."

"When she gets one, who looks after the children?"

Was this another trick question or was I getting paranoid? I tried not to snap as I replied.

"I do of course."

"What about when you are at work?"

"Both children attend school so its not really a problem. I have an understanding employer. They know about Jane's illness and realise that raising children comes with difficulties. If I need time off I can take it."

I cringed; what had I just said? I had let my guard down and admitted to problems. Saunders either did not hear or chose to ignore the remark. Or perhaps she had made a mental note for future reference.

"Isn't Tom too young for school?"

"Its a pre-school. We have to pay for it. Its important for Tom's development."

"Ah, yes, I see. Of course. Does your wife pick them up from school?"

I was starting to get very annoyed with the inquisition. Was she trying to trick me into saying something I would regret?

"What point are you trying to make?"

"I am simply trying to understand the environment in which the children are living. Their day to day lives are important. If your wife has continuing illness problems then it is of concern. What if she is unwell and unable to pick them up? We may be able to help. There are agencies that can offer support."

I was suddenly overwhelmed with a sense of resentment at her presence. This was serious. One word out of place, one ill conceived thought on my part and the consequences could be unthinkable. Perhaps this line of questioning was also intended to expose any issues with me as well. My resentment grew at the thought and turned to anger. I had read about these dreadful people and the awful mistakes they made. They had extensive powers and often tore families apart on the smallest pretext. I vowed this would not happen to my family.

I suddenly realised I was staring at Saunders with what was almost certainly an unfriendly and hostile face. This fear was confirmed as she tried to defuse the situation. She tried to smile and re-assure me.

"What I have just seen is two very contented and level headed children and a caring father. I know how tough it is bringing up young children and holding down a full time job. If there is anything we can do to help you with any small problems your wife is having then let me know. We are on your side."

Her words made me feel chastised rather than comforted and my anger grew. I was being patronised. I felt like I was in some cheap soap opera.

"You will have to excuse me soon. I have to get the children's tea ready."

"Of course. Do they both eat well?"

As the inquisition continued I was struggling to maintain my calm.

"Yes. They both have healthy appetites. Now was there anything else?"

"No, I think we are done thank you."

Saunders stood and offered her hand. So physical contact was permitted in her line of work. Or perhaps she had concluded that I was not a threat. Clutching at straws I convinced myself that it was a good sign. Staring at her hand for a few seconds I decided that it would be advisable to accept it and shook meekly. The insincerity must have been obvious.

In business we put great store in people's handshakes. It said a lot about them. Mine was not saying great things about me. It was indecisive and insincere.

In the hallway as she struggled to put her still damp coat on I looked at her with disdain. Angry thoughts raced around my head. My taxes paid for these interfering busy bodies but they had the weight of law behind them. It was democracy in action. I hand over the money, they tell me what to do. My head raced with irrational thoughts. I did not vote for this. I did not vote for my own destruction.

Returning to the front room to my surprise the children were still playing the silly game. I had expected them to have disappeared, Angela to her room and Tom to whatever mischief he could find. They were keeping up the pretence admirably.

Jane looked at me intently. To my immense annoyance she had decided to come to life. It was too late now; the damage had been done.

"Who was that awful woman?"

Once again Jane was acting as if nothing had happened. Was this constant deleting of events another effect of her illness? Was the part of her brain responsible for assimilating events damaged? It would have been a comfort to believe this but I was inclined to believe a more sinister explanation. She was ignoring things that were uncomfortable as if ignoring them meant they did not happen.

"You know who she was. She was a welfare officer checking up on us."

"Why was she checking up on you? What have you done?"

It was getting worse. She was detaching herself from her actions. Worse still, she kept putting the blame on me. Her mental state was becoming increasingly fragile. Perhaps these welfare people had a point. I rejected the thought angrily. It was none of their damn business how I looked after my family. This family was my responsibility not some hideous social services organisation. I would find an answer to this chaos without their interference.

~ 10 ~

Opening her eyes slowly Jane looked around the darkened room. As she tried to rise from the hard and unpleasantly smelling bed, pain shot through her head as it started to spin. Collapsing again she took slow and deliberate deep breaths. She measured each breath as it slowly revived her, refreshing her dulled senses. The sound of her own breathing hurt her ears as her head throbbed. As the pain subsided she looked around again at the unfamiliar surroundings.

A second attempt to sit up was less painful and the spinning less severe. As her head started to clear her eyes began to focus more clearly. Where was she? Ragged curtains hung across the window. The bare floor boards were dirty and covered in marks and stains. In the far corner a dark damp patch was working its way down from the ceiling. It seemed to fit perfectly with the room. A smell of decay filled the air. Vague sounds of voices and traffic drifted into the room assailing her aching head.

A scruffy unkempt woman entered the room and spoke with a voice damaged by too much smoking.

She could barely utter a few words before coughing. Her accent was uncultured and lazy. Speaking was too much effort.

"Come on. You've had your fun. Time to go."

"What fun? Go where?"

"To wherever you call home love. And if you don't remember what happened it ain't my problem. Come on, we need the room. We have another paying customer waiting. Here, take your things."

Jane swung her legs to the floor as she sat up. Pain surged once more through her head and she started to shake. An intolerant voice chastised her.

"Don't just sit there. Get moving."

An explosive cough caused the woman to convulse alarmingly. Impatiently she waved her arm in the direction of the open door. As Jane shuffled unsteadily towards the door the woman looked her up and down with disgust.

"I was going to show you where the toilet is but its too late."

Jane looked down to see the damp patch on her dress. A feeling of shame overwhelmed her. She trudged slowly down a poorly lit stairway and out into the street. Statuesque she stood looking around her trying to make sense of her surroundings. Conscious of the damp in her mid region she tried to hide in a doorway. Tired, confused, in pain and embarrassed she sat down.

I had taken a day off work and driven Jane at the local surgery at nine o'clock. They were going to run a few tests that could take several hours. I left her there to take the kids to school. Ignoring their patronising suspicions that I was being paranoid I had insisted that I was still concerned about her. To my mind she did not seem to be improving. Physically she was becoming weaker and was given to even more frequent headaches. But of most concern was that she was still this stranger who treated us with little care or concern. The sickness in her mind was distressing and I wanted answers.

It was mid afternoon when the phone rang. I had started to worry about how long Jane had been at the surgery but with the sound of the ringing my concern vanished. It must have been the surgery calling to tell me Jane was ready to come home. I answered with anticipation.

"Hello. Runton 6598."

Why did I still use this old number? The exchange had been digitalised twenty years ago. We humans can be creatures of habit.

"Mister Cotter? Detective Roberts, Runton police. We have your wife in the station. Could you..."

"What? I don't understand. What do you mean?"

"Your wife was found wandering the streets. She is alright but a little confused. Can you come and collect her? We could send her home in one of our cars but she is a little distressed. She won't let anyone get near her. Perhaps you could come and calm her down."

"Why is she there? Has she done anything wrong?"

"Not really. She's well, how can I put it? She's in a bit of a state."

"State? What do you mean? What do you mean not really?"

“It would be best if you could come Sir and I can explain.”

“Of course. I will be there in about ten minutes. I just need to sort the kids out. Please tell Jane I am coming.”

It was getting near time to collect Tom from pre-school and Angela from school. I had to do this before sorting out whatever had happened to Jane. They were my priority. I was obsessed with making sure that Jane's problems had minimal impact on them. It was a tough struggle but I was determined. I was running out of energy but found enough for the important things.

At the police station I left the kids sit in reception under the watchful eye of the custody Sergeant. A family man himself he was more than willing and kept them entertained pulling faces and making strange noises. He would raise his finger high in the air, twirl it around and bring it down stabbing the keyboard. His face would then light up with surprise as the screen beeped and he would emit a shriek of delight..

Detective Roberts ushered me through to a small room presumably used for interviews. Was this an ominous sign?

“Please sit Mister Cotter. I would just like a few words before we bring your wife out.”

“Out?”

“She's in one of the cells. Its not locked. Its the only accommodation we have I'm afraid. This isn't a hotel. She's OK. She's calmed down a bit now. She was very agitated but we could not understand what she was saying. She kept going on about a dark man. Does that mean anything to you?"

It did but I was not going to admit it to this stranger.

"No. So what happened? You sounded worried on the phone. When I asked you if she had done anything wrong you replied: not really. What did you mean?"

"We believe she may have been into one of the local drug dens."

"What makes you think that?"

"We found her wandering in the Black District."

"The Black District? I've never heard of it."

"Its on the Downback Estate to the South of the town. Its where all the drug dealers and addicts hang out. Its part of an initiative to try to contains drugs. In effect we put a fence round the area and let them get on with it. It keeps the problem out of the wider area. We keep a close eye on what is going on and that's why we found your wife. We know the faces of pretty much everyone there so as a stranger she stood out. She did not fit the mould of an dealer or addict."

"My wife has never taken drugs."

"I'm afraid the police doctor found a tell tale mark on her left arm. We had to call him in to check she was alright."

"She has been to the doctors today. Are you sure it was not from them taking a blood sample?"

"Its not in the usual place and it is rather too clumsy. It looks like someone has stabbed a needle in rather roughly and bruised a muscle. The doctor took a blood sample and it tested positive."

Chaos broke out in my head so much so that the questions I wanted to ask would not form. Perhaps Roberts could sense my panic as he calmly answered all my unasked questions.

"Your wife seems to remember nothing about what happened. The doctor says she is unharmed. The wound is clean and not infected. Did she have any money on her?"

"Yes, some, in a small handbag. About forty pounds I think."

"I see. Well she has the bag. That's how we managed to find out who she was and contact you. But there is no money in it."

"So was she robbed?"

"Its a nasty area. When they rob someone there tends to be a lot more damage. There are usually assault wounds. And they would almost certainly have taken the bag and jewellery. Your wife has wedding and engagement rings on. These would usually be taken. I am sorry to ask this but could she have deliberately gone to the estate for drugs?"

I hesitated considering my response. In truth I was no longer surprised at anything Jane did but this was several steps too far.

"I don't believe so, no. In fact definitely no. She despises everything about drugs. She is even reluctant to takes a pill for a headache."

"Does she suffer from blackouts or periods where she is not aware of her behaviour?"

Again I felt compelled to lie. I had a duty to protect Jane. I also had a duty to protect the children. It was essential that I showed Jane to be as normal as possible. That damn welfare woman was still lurking in the background. I was convinced she was just waiting for any excuse to intervene.

"No. We have two children. It would be dangerous if she suffered such things."

"I see. You say she was visiting the doctor. Was it the South Runtorn Surgery?"

"Yes, why?"

"It is quite close to the Downback Estate. May I ask what she visited the surgery for?"

"Just a routine check up. The practice gives us one each year."

Lie upon lie was building. Was I carrying it off or did I look nervous? Roberts stood and started to walk towards the door. Perhaps he had heard enough lies.

"OK. Look, we will bring your wife through and you can take her home. If she remembers anything of what happened you can call me on this number."

I took the card being offered.

"Are you expecting her to remember anything?"

Shrugging his shoulders Roberts left without replying. It was a contemptuous gesture. He had obviously made up his mind about Jane and had better things to do than waste his time with me and this stupid woman. Junkies were a waste of police time.

I sat dazed and confused trying to tell my head to calm down. Several minutes later a policewoman entered the room gently leading Jane by the arm. As I stood she beamed a friendly smile.

"Here you are Mrs Cotter. As we promised, your husband is here to take you home."

Jane looked at me with a distant stare. Her eyes were dark with swelling around them. Suddenly they widened and the merest hint of a smile appeared on her lips. It was the first time she had smiled since we had returned from Kenya. I returned the smile but hers disappeared instantly. Had it actually been there or was I fooling myself? Did I imagine something I desperately wanted to see?

In reception the children were sitting quietly watching the activity of the busy station. As Jane and I approached they got up and ran over to us. With his usual lack of subtlety Tom called the world as he saw it.

"Is weird Mummy in trouble? What did she do? Will she be on the television? Did she have her fingerprints taken?"

Jane scowled at Tom who retreated behind me and peered at Jane from behind my legs. Weird mummy did not look pleased.

"No Tom. Mummy just got lost coming back from the Doctor. These nice men found her and now we are taking her home."

Tom seemed satisfied and stepped out from behind the shelter of my legs.

"Ah that's good then."

He was staring intently at Jane's hands looking for signs of black ink. In all this uncertainty he managed to maintain his innocence. Angela on the other hand had a look of deep concern.

Jane said nothing on the drive home and once indoors I could not summons the courage to ask her anything about what had happened. I knew that in all probability she would either not respond or fly off the handle. Perhaps if I left her to her own thoughts she would speak later. I was however absolutely determined to speak to the Surgery to find out what happened. They had a duty of care which they had abdicated.

Evening surgery started at six o'clock and at precisely two minutes after six I telephoned. I recognised the voice of the receptionist, a typical no nonsense strictly practical woman. Given the awkward behaviour of many patients she was ideal for the job but difficult to deal with. She treated everyone as a nuisance and inconvenience.

"South Runtorn Practice. How may I help?"

"Its Andrew Cotter. My wife was in this morning for some tests. Someone was supposed to tell me when you had finished with her so I could come and collect her. The police found her up wandering the streets. What the hell happened?"

"I would thank you not to swear Mister Roberts. All calls are recorded. We do not tolerate abuse."

I could barely contain my anger. She was a damn jobs worth more concerned about my language than patient care.

"Look, I left my wife in your care and the next thing I know the police have picked her up. I have every right to be annoyed. I want an explanation."

The phone went silent and I waited impatiently for a response. If they had cut me off I would go there in person and they would really hear some bad language. There was a click and I heard the voice of the receptionist.

"According to our notes your wife said she was going to order a taxi and find her own way home."

They had been sensible enough to make notes, why? Were they concerned? And why had they ignored my instructions? Had they not made a note of those?

"But I specifically said she was not to be allowed home on her own and that I would collect her."

"She is a responsible adult Mister Cotter. You gave us no cause to suppose she was not capable. It says nothing in her notes to that effect. My colleague says Mrs Roberts was calm and seemed very responsible. We had no cause for concern."

Suddenly there was a crash from the kitchen. I needed to investigate.

"Well there was plenty of room for concern. I am not happy with this. It is not the last you have heard of it."

I angrily slammed down the phone. None of this made sense. In the weeks we had been home Jane had not shown any sense of responsibility. She had seemed like a lost soul, bad tempered, confused and helpless. How could they have seen any different or was Jane capable of changing to suit her situation? If true this would be a worrying development.

In the kitchen Tom was looking sheepish. I looked down to see a broken glass on the floor near him. Jane was staring at the mess transfixed by the sparkling pieces of glass. She moved her head from side to side watching as the light caught each piece differently..

"What have you done?"

"It slipped."

What was he doing with a glass? We only allowed him a plastic cup. I should have been annoyed but my mind was still wrestling with what had happened today.

“Come on. Let's clear it up before someone cuts themselves.”

Jane was slowly shaking her head.

“Its not such a mess as that place.”

I listened intently. Was Jane about to talk about what happened?

“What place?”

“Nowhere. I was just thinking out loud. Are you going to clear this up? That boy is a nuisance.”

With a dismissive shrug Jane left the kitchen. Tom was on the verge of tears so I tried to comfort him.

“Its alright. Let's clear this up.”

“But you said I must not touch glass.”

“If you are very very careful you can help me pick up some of the pieces.”

As he bent down to pick up a large piece he mumbled to himself.

“Mummy's weird.”

~ 11 ~

As a concerned parent I had always kept a close eye on the kids activities online. A career IT specialist, I had grown up with computers and had a deep knowledge of technology. It was almost a daily task for me to sort out all manner of problems with our computers, the network, the printer, the email that would not send, the application that would not open, and just about anything that was technology based. I was expected to respond immediately and effectively to the plaintive cries of: *dad, there's something wrong, or its not working*. Typically the children tried to ignore me most of the time but demanded my full attention when they wanted something. I knew my place.

Recently I had grown increasingly concerned at the way technology was now being used. Giant global money making organisations were exploiting technology almost without restraint and certainly without any strict moral control. I was also acutely aware of the dangers especially those associated with social media and determined that the children would not fall foul of it. I would not let my children be bullied by other children or fall prey to all kinds of perverts that stalked the Internet.

I had read the worrying statistics. Nearly half of all web site accesses were for pornography. There were billion messages a day on social networks of which a quarter of were malicious. People were increasingly spending time in virtual worlds rather than the real world. This was seriously hampering their social development. Their interpersonal skills were poor and their ability to communicate effectively severely damaged. One of the most significant advances in mankind's history was shifting us into a new dark age. Man always seemed to find an evil use for everything. In my mind technology was taking our civilisation backwards.

There was a recent item in the news about a drop in teenage pregnancies in the UK because the kids were spending more time on social networks rather than meeting people and doing, well, what they were doing before to get pregnant. Though this was obviously a positive outcome it did raise an underlying concern about the lack of interaction with people. Teenagers would rather talk to a screen than a real person. It was easier, required less effort and did not tell them to stop what they were doing. They could give voice to their immature thoughts without censure. There was no need for the restraint of civil interaction.

Another concern was their physical health. Research based on long term users suggested that being sat crouched over a keyboard and staring at a screen had a detrimental effect on health. Our bodies are meant to move and if they spend too long being inactive there are consequences. As a long term user myself I was starting to see signs of physical problems. I had developed a curvature of the spine that was having implications for my general health.

I had put various personal health problems down to age but that was only part of the story. As a child before the computer age I had been very active and yet in later life was starting to suffer. How much more risk is associated with less active kids? What would be the long term damage for children who had not led the sort of active childhood I had?

Having painstakingly set up all the appropriate controls and activated all the safeguards I could I was reasonably content that my family were protected from what I saw as the growing evil of the Internet. The children would simply have to learn how to cope with peer pressure and not indulge in the things that I saw as potentially harmful. It was a question of trust. They needed to trust that I knew what was best for them. I was sure they would thank me one day.

I could not do much about the amount of time the children spent on their computers. There was a line between being a concerned parent and a spoilsport which I tried studiously not to cross. I did not want the children to start to hate me because I always stopped them enjoying themselves. How could I spend my whole day earning a living from computers only to stop the kids using them? It would appear to their simple eyes to be a blatant act of hypocrisy and would compromise their respect for me. But we had reached an agreement. The kids were allowed to use their computers so long as they had done certain tasks. In effect usage was a reward for good behaviour. It was probably the best compromise I could hope for.

I had noticed that of late Angela had been spending more time than usual on her computer. She had kept to the agreement and done all the things expected of her so I had no cause to challenge her. It would only have caused an argument and probably resulted in tears. She was growing up fast. She had learnt that I had a soft heart and that tears were an effective weapon. But I was concerned and needed to find out what was fascinating her so much. Every time I subtly tried to find out what she was up to she was evasive. In the past she had been excited and proud to tell me what she was doing. Now she never spoke about it and ignored my questions. I knew evasion was a warning sign so my fears deepened.

It was getting late and close to Angela's bed time. I entered her room to see her crouched over the keyboard in the way that harboured concerns for long term health: spine curved unnaturally, shoulders hunched and stomach compressed.

"You're working late. What are you up to? Anything interesting?"

Without looking up Angela continued typing.

"Chatting with Robert."

My concerned instincts suddenly flared up but I tried not to sound agitated. I did not want to alert her to my concern and put her on the defensive.

"Who is Robert?"

"One of Mummy's friends."

Jane and I shared friends. I had never heard of Robert. I was certain that with Jane's current insular behaviour she would not have made any new friends unless it was on-line. It was on-line friends that worried me. There was so much predatory low life prowling social networks and chat rooms. There were guidelines about children under thirteen using social networks. In fact I had a suspicion it was illegal but how could anyone police what was happening abroad? Policing absolutely had to start with the parents. But peer pressure was dictating my actions. All her friends chatted on line how could I ban her?

I knew that a direct challenge to Angela would get me nowhere so decided on a subtle approach. I would show some interest.

"What are you chatting about?"

Angela clicked on the mouse and a different screen appeared.

"Nothing just silly things."

I looked hard at her face, was she hiding something? Was that smile one of embarrassment or genuine pleasure at seeing me? It was becoming ever harder to read her face. She was losing her simple naivety. Of course this happens as children get older but she was still only eleven. She should still look innocent.

I tried to use my calmest most persuasive voice. In truth it probably sounded more nagging than anything.

"It's getting late. Perhaps you should be thinking about stopping and getting ready for bed."

With a final click the screen went blank and Angela stood up. I watched as she unfurled her body slowly and with a twinge. She was eleven years old but looked like a little old lady. Was she starting to show signs of physical problems already? I needed to think about this. As a parent I had a duty to give my kids the best start in life even if they objected. Even if they resented me now they would thank me in later life. They never told me about this in the small print of parenthood.

I had encouraged her to take an interest in computers. It was after all my life and the way I earned a living. Like it or not computers were an integral part of our lives. Excluding her from this would be wrong. I now needed to persuade her that they also caused harm.

Much as I would have liked to restrict their usage more strictly I was facing an impossible battle. Their school was using computers more and I knew that peer pressure meant she needed to chat to her friends. Angela had told me that there was an unwritten law of social media that said if you were not chatting with people they were probably talking about you. And it is a sad inevitability that when kids talk about other kids it is usually in derogatory terms. Social media had actually made this problem worse. They felt they could chat more freely than face to face and were therefore more uninhibited. With the constraints of physical interaction missing their minds were much freer to create mischievous thoughts.

This small incident made me resolve to investigate what she was doing. I had set a precedent of checking all three of our computers every so often for bugs and other problems. I also tweaked the performance, backed up essential files and deleted all the junk that inevitably accumulates. In practice this was essential to enable me to sort out the mess the machines usually ended up in. If I was lucky I pre-empted problems by catching them early but more typically I was fire-fighting. Children abuse computers as much as they abuse other toys.

Significantly, this regular exercise created a plausible and acceptable way for me to check without the children thinking I was spying on them. Angela was wise enough to understand I was probably checking but accepted that it was the price for my bailing her out every so often. She had started to learn that life was about give and take. If she wanted something from me there was a price.

I had shown Angela how to password protect the computer. It stopped Tom playing with it. She had always told me the password so that I could fix any problems. And I was ever willing to respond to the frequent plaintive cry of 'Daddy, its not working.' But early afternoon the following day when she was at school I tried to activate her computer and the sign-on screen rejected the password. She had changed it without telling me. I hesitated to think the worst. Perhaps she had just forgotten. I rejected this possibility. She always told me what the password was. We wrote it down in the black book that contained all critical information. How otherwise could I fix any mess? But my mind was walking a tight rope swaying one way and another. What was she hiding?

So much had happened recently that I was losing touch with the grounding in my life. In an uncertain world I lived by certainties but these were fast vanishing to be replaced by a fog of constant doubts. Things no longer proceeded in a controlled order. They sprang at me, challenging me.

How was I to handle this? Though Angela had made no reference to the incident when Jane struck her perhaps it had left a lasting legacy. What she did not need was for her father to be heavy handed. I absolutely had to be the good cop.

Once again my feelings towards Jane were mixed and confused. She had so much to answer for. Her behaviour was having a profound and damaging impact on the children. My mind strayed to the visit of the welfare worker and her guarded questions about Jane. Was this precisely what she was concerned about? Did she consider that my children were at risk? The thought stung me heavily. I really did need to find out what Angela was doing. I would handle the fallout as best I could.

Early the following morning I confronted Angela as once again she was chatting on-line.

"I need to check you machine for viruses. There's a new one that wrecks the hard drive. It comes via social media."

Without looking up Angela dismissed my suggestion.

"I ran a virus scan earlier. Everything is OK."

I stood confused and dismayed. I had told a lie, where could I go now, another lie? I had no choice but to play the heavy handed father.

"I insist on doing it. I'm not going to waste my time fixing a wrecked hard drive."

Angela sighed impatiently and glared at me.

"You are a pain Dad."

"What's the new password? I'll check the machine while you are eating breakfast."

"Just give me a minute. I'll leave it switched on."

Angela clattered furiously on the keyboard. What was she covering up?

"What are you doing?"

"Just signing off from the chat room."

I looked at her face as she typed. It was a picture of simple innocence. Was I mistrusting her without reason? I felt a sense of shame which only grew when I discovered nothing untoward on her laptop.

~ 12 ~

I had always thought that self harming was something teenagers did as they struggled with the physical and emotional changes of growing up. Common opinion holds that it is a cry for help and that usually they grow out of it as experience and maturity grow with them. As their mental capacity grows they are more able to cope with the stresses that life imposes on them.

For those of us who have not self harmed it is difficult to understand. I took a dismissive view. It was a cowardly act that left others to suffer and pick up the pieces. Coping with life's difficulties was part of growing up. Developing a coping mechanism was essential. No one should flounder. There was enough help around if you really needed it. It was just a matter of asking. But it is a characteristic of depression that the sufferer ceases to communicate. Its a destructive cycle. Without interaction their depression deepens.

My own teenage years had not been particularly enjoyable. Rather than getting drunk and behaving as so many teenagers do I mostly was restrained and studied to better myself. This contrasted with my peers who thought they were already clever enough and did not need to bother bettering themselves. They were already perfect, knew it all and the world was theirs. I was not so sure. So much of life seemed difficult and contradictory. My self confidence matured slowly. It was a calculated progression as I learned from experience. Each test life set me was faced and lessons carefully learnt.

My behaviour was a source of some concern to my parents. It was if they actually wanted me to misbehave so they could chastise me like my siblings. I was a disappointment. It must have frustrated them. All that pent up disapproval they could not give vent to. But at no time in my struggles to adulthood did I feel the urge to self harm. Any anger I felt was towards others not myself. I had several moments where I wanted to inflict punishment on other people but never on myself.

Given my intolerant attitude to self harming I was to receive an uncomfortable shock. Jane's continuing unbalanced mind led her to begin to self harm. The first time was when I returned home from work one day to find Angela sitting on the sofa next to Jane who was bleeding from a cut on her arm.

I thought nothing of it at first. Jane had continued to be a little unsteady and clumsy and I cringed on occasions when I saw her handling a knife. She had taken to preparing meals though in practice I usually had to finish the work and clean up the mess. I assumed that my fears had been realised and she had slipped. As I held Jane's arm to exam the cut I looked at Angela's frightened face.

"What happened?"

"Mummy cut herself."

"Yes, I can see that but how did it happen?"

Angela made a strange motion with her hand but the meaning was clear. Jane had done it deliberately. A tear trickled down Angela's face as she looked at me with despair.

My reaction was one of anger. How could Jane put Angela though this? These were the formative years of her young life. They would shape her character and the things that happened would stay with her for the rest of her life. I had tried so hard to build a safe environment for the children and taken great care to ensure they experienced the positive things of life. Isn't that what all parents are supposed to do? Jane was undoing all the work but much worse, she was causing damage and she seemed not to care.

As I sat still holding Jane's arm I became aware that another emotion was building inside. It was the first shoots of a profound hatred. I was starting to hate Jane. How could this happen? Wasn't I supposed to be concerned and caring about her condition? Weren't we supposed to be together in sickness and in health? But this woman was not the Jane I knew. I was ceasing to care about her. It somehow seemed acceptable to feel hatred for this woman who was wrecking my children's lives. They say self harming is a cry for help. This seemed more like a malicious action to cause harm to others.

My thoughts were disturbed by Angela's timid concerned voice.

"Are we going to call the doctor Daddy?"

"No. It's only a small cut. We can fix it."

I was sure my words sounded unconvincing but I did not want to get anyone else involved. Our situation was already difficult and the social worker was starting to ask even more questions. She had come to the house once when I was not there. Jane had reacted with hostility and refused to let her in. It was apparent that she was becoming increasingly concerned about Jane and I did not want to provide her with more ammunition. When I was present Jane did talk to this woman who was annoying her. On more than one occasion I was forced to intervene as Jane started to become hostile towards the social worker.

Angela gave me a strange look. Though of tender years she was growing up fast. My reassurances were carrying less and less weight. She accepted my decision but her mind was asking questions which surfaced with a plaintive plea.

"But she did this on purpose, shouldn't we tell someone?"

I looked at Jane who continued to sit motionless apparently asleep. Was she listening as we talked about her in the third person? Isn't that how people talked about a disabled person? Does she take sugar? We were starting to treat Jane less as a mother and wife and more like a detached person staying in our home. We had become carers for her. We were caring for this sick stranger.

"She is not well Angela. We need to give her time to recover."

Even I did not believe what I was saying but nothing more constructive came to mind. I had developed an ostrich mentality. Let's pretend everything is alright and it will all go away. Angela stood up and walked slowly out of the room. Glancing back over her shoulder I saw her face contorted and distressed. What damage had this done to her young impressionable mind?

Later when Jane had gone to bed I sat once again in front of the television watching I had no idea what. Were we now in the situation that I could not go to work and trust that something bad not would happen? A terrifying thought entered my head. Jane had harmed herself, what if next she harmed one of the children? She had already struck Angela and was under suspicion of causing other harm. Rather than recovering her mind seemed to be degenerating. How far would she go? I felt an overwhelming cocktail of helplessness, anxiety and despair. It was a feeling I had no idea how to handle.

I spent the following day at work worrying. I imagined a number of terrible things that I desperately tried to bury. Whatever monster Jane was turning into she was still the children's mother. Surely there was still some vestige of maternal instinct that would act as a check on her behaviour?

I returned home full of trepidation. But all was well. Jane seemed in a relaxed outgoing mood and the house was full of the characteristic noises children make whatever they are doing. It appeared that I was returning once again to a happy family. Dare I believe it?

It was over a week later that Jane self harmed again. This time she had cut herself on a pair of secateurs whilst tinkering in the garden. Once again my immediate reaction was that it had been a simple accident but Angela's face told me different. Etched on her young features once more was that frightened uncertain look.

Jane was sitting in the kitchen watching the blood slowly trickle from her arm onto the floor. It was as if the drips had hypnotised her and she was in a trance. I looked to Angela who was holding a tea towel uncertain as to what to do. Was she scared of Jane? I also noticed Tom standing in the door to the hall. His look was more of childish curiosity. This was something new. What was going on? I felt an odd sense of relief that at least Jane's behaviour was not badly affecting him. He still saw the world as exciting and full of adventure,

One incident I could ignore. It could have been accidental couldn't it? Angela could have been mistaken couldn't she? Could the second incident have been an accident? These questions were answered starkly when I personally witnessed her third attempt to harm herself.

Tom had been playing with one of his toy lorries on the kitchen work top and had accidentally knocked a plate onto the floor. As I entered the kitchen to see what had happened Jane bent down and started to pick up the pieces. With one larger piece she nicked her left wrist. I could see it was deliberate by her odd behaviour. She quickly looked up to see if anyone had noticed.

For the third time I was obliged to stem the blood flow and patch up the mess. This was now becoming serious. This was beyond my coping. I really needed help. I needed to talk to someone. The visit to the doctors surgery had been a disaster. Jane still had not spoken about what happened. Was her current behaviour related to it? Had something happened that had made her suicidal? Before I had a chance to do anything, events overtook me with a crushing force.

~ 13 ~

I was awoken at six o'clock by a loud and urgent banging on the front door. I sat up listening intently but the house was in silence. Was I dreaming? I had been having a lot of disturbing dreams lately. Anything was possible. A second louder and more urgent bang told me I was not dreaming. Incautiously rising too rapidly I paused to allow my head to stop spinning, pulled on my dressing gown and walked onto the landing. Angela was standing in the doorway of her bedroom looking very scared.

"Have they come to take us away Daddy?"

"What? What do you mean? No. Nobody is going to take you away. Go back into your room."

As I walked downstairs a third even more urgent series of bangs rattled the front door. Whoever was banging was becoming impatient. Approaching cautiously I opened the door and peered round ready to ward off anything untoward. In the entrance stood a slightly scruffy man in a grey suit with three uniformed policemen close behind. He spoke calmly and without emotion.

"Mister Cotter?"

"Yes."

Thrusting a piece of paper close to my face the man spoke more harshly. It was a commanding and compelling voice that startled my sleepy brain.

"Detective Sergeant Vinall, I have a warrant to search your house."

I was stunned. It was like something I had seen on television.

"What for? What are you looking for?"

"We believe child pornography has emanated from this address."

I was not sure whether I was still half asleep or simply not believing what I was hearing but I stood staring at the man in silence. Child pornography had been in and out of the news for months and I knew there was a large police operation across the country. The scale and extent of the offence had been alarming. Many people had been arrested and more were under investigation. In such a big operation there would be mistakes. This was obviously one of them.

Personal experience had shown me it was easy to trip over a questionable web site accidentally. The most innocent of searches could come up with undesirable results. Only recently I had searched for a specific software company and been presented with a gay web site in Amsterdam with explicit pictures. I had spotted it and ignored it but despite my experience I had naively clicked on some awful sites. These low life were adept at hiding things in apparently innocent wrappers ready to trap the careless. It was a ploy to awaken curiosity.

There was a bustle of activity behind the detective as I stood as if in a trance. It was an unreal situation I was struggling to understand. My brain finally woke up and entered a state of disbelief.

"That's absurd. There must be some mistake."

Brushing past me Vinall beckoned the policemen to follow. Looking all around he spoke coarsely into the hallway ahead of him.

"We can discuss this later at the station. For now my officers are here to search the house."

As if halted by a sudden thought he stopped and turned to look at me. He nodded his head nodded in the direction of the stairs.

"I believe there are children in the house?"

"Yes, my daughter and son."

Satisfied he signalled to a policewoman who was standing near the front gate at the end of the pathway. Instantly the woman walked quickly towards us. Without a word she walked upstairs whilst the detective kept an attentive watch on me for any sign of resistance. I felt powerless but retained enough wit to realise that creating a fuss would make matters worse. My mind wandered to Angela and the scared look on her face. What had she meant about people coming to take them away? She had said 'us' which I presumed referred to her and Tom. Why had I dismissed her concern so readily as nonsense? What had she meant? I wanted to go and talk to her but my way was barred by Sergeant Vinall.

I stood watching the scene of chaos as the policemen searched the house. One by one all three of our computers were carried past me and out of the front door. Several files of paperwork swiftly followed.

Then came my digital camera. They had obviously been rifling through the study I had so carefully protected from Tom's interference.

As each item passed Sergeant Vinall made a note on a clipboard and made an expression that could best be describe as a look of satisfaction. For a fleeting moment I was almost impressed with their efficiency. The realisation that this was my house and these were my possessions quickly dispelled the illusion. Police efficiency should have been furthermost from my mind. Was I starting to pick up Jane's habit of being detached from reality?

After a few minutes I heard a commotion and the raised voice of Jane upstairs. A second policewoman had appeared from somewhere and was leading Jane downstairs by the arm. Jane was scowling at her and struggling in vain to control her simmering temper. As they passed me Jane looked at me and shouted angrily.

"What is going on? What have you done?"

I could think of no reply that made sense so kept silent. I felt a deep resentment that Jane was accusing me. How could she believe I was capable of such an awful thing? If the police were right then Jane must have been the culprit. How could she be capable of such a thing? None of it made sense. My thoughts were disturbed by Vinall.

"I need any mobile phones."

"What for?"

Vinall ignored my question and looked me up and down.

"You need to go and get dressed sir. I would like you to come with us."

I suddenly became aware of standing in front of these strangers in just my dressing gown. I felt vulnerable and a little silly. We were being accused of peddling pornography and I was standing in front of strangers with virtually no clothes on.

Upstairs I hastily dressed and went towards Angela's bedroom. Inside the children were sitting on the bed whilst the policewoman stood nearby. As I approached she swiftly held up her hand barring my way.

"I am sorry sir you cannot come in. You can see the children later at the station."

In my head conflict raged. I wanted to protest but realised it would not help the situation. The policewoman had her hand poised over her radio ready to summons help. It was an unnecessary caution. I would not and could not attack a woman however angry I was. But surely she could recognise a father's instinct to protect his children?

I took a step backwards still peering anxiously into the room. Angela and Tom looked at me with expressions that hurt deeply. They were confused and scared and my helplessness in coming to their aid was making it worse. If their father could not protect them who could?

After swiftly dragging on whatever clothes came to hand I stormed downstairs to where the sergeant still stood supervising operations.

"Am I under arrest?"

Involuntarily he jerked his head back at my aggression. Dealing with aggressive and violent people must be one of the hazards of the job. He no doubt recognised signs of aggression and reacted accordingly.

"No Sir. But it would be helpful if you would come with us to answer some questions. And we need an appropriate adult to accompany the children."

I should have told them what to do with their ridiculous accusation but my confused mind could think of no other response than meek compliance. My logical training was telling me that I needed to have a deeper understanding of what was going on until I could react with any reason. It made no sense to rage at something I did not fully understand.

They might have had questions but I had more pressing ones that needed answers. I dallied trying to decide whether to be awkward or co-operate. In an instant the decision was made as I saw the children outside being marshalled into a police car. I had to go with them. I could not leave them alone in the hands of these people.

In my concern for the children I had all but forgotten about Jane who had been forcefully put into a van and driven away. She had put up a fight scratching and kicking at the policewoman and policeman trying to restrain her. I did not recognise the wild animal that was supposed to be my wife and was sickened as the reality of our situation sunk in.

In a matter of a minute I was left alone in the house with detective Vinall who was patiently waiting for me to finish collecting my things. The chaos of a few minutes earlier seemed unreal, but the implications of what had happened were most definitely naked reality.

~ 14 ~

At the station Jane and I were shown into separate interview rooms whilst the children were led away by the same policewoman that had been so protective of them at the house. On reflection she seemed pleasant enough and the children were calm so I felt at least some small measure of relief.

I was clutching at straws. I was a realist, I never clutched at straws. Everything in life for me was black or white. I was being swept along by events beyond both my control and comprehension so anything I could cling on to was welcome. At that precise moment any straws would do. A friendly policewoman was taking care of the children, shielding them from the hell breaking around them.

As he was led away Tom was pleading with the policewoman to have his fingerprints taken like they do on television. I marvelled at his childish innocence. Even in the midst of disaster he found something to interest and amuse him. I noticed later the tell tale black smudges on his hands that told of the success of his pleading. I was reassured by the policewoman that they had not kept his fingerprints but destroyed them when he had gone.

In fact as I learnt when mine were taken they used electronic fingerprinting rather than ink so she had gone out of her way to accommodate Tom. I was grateful for her show of kindness amid the harshness of our situation. Tom would now have an adventure to tell his friends about. I was suddenly overwhelmed by the thought of what people would think. I could keep silent but Tom most certainly could not. Had I not told the children they should not have secrets? He was bound to boast of his adventure.

As I sat in the interview room confused and anxious two men entered in plain clothes. The younger of the two introduced himself as Detective Barclay and introduced his colleague as Inspector Jones. Sitting opposite on the other side of a small well worn table covered with stains from numerous cups Barclay spoke coldly and harshly.

"I will come straight to the point sir. We have clear evidence of child pornography being posted on-line from a computer in your house. Our labs will check the computers to clarify the proof but we are pretty sure they will find it. We know your wife is involved. She made no pretence of trying to hide her identity. She even signed some of the clips and talked about her children. What we need to establish is whether you had any involvement."

It was one of those moments when something is so alien you have no idea how to respond. That someone could even think that I would be so perverted was beyond my comprehension. How can you respond to something that makes no sense to you? Rage does not make for clear thinking. I paused in silence trying to calm down. If I showed my anger it would suit their purposes. I could not surrender complete control to them. Calmness bought clarity to my thinking.

"Do I need to have a solicitor present? Your accusation is completely unacceptable."

"Of course that is your right but I am not accusing you of anything. I am simply asking if you had any knowledge of your wife's activities. If you have nothing to hide then the question is perfectly innocent."

The patronising edge to his voice irritated me. This was not a matter to be so flippant about. Try as I might I could not control my anger.

"No it damn well is not! You are suggesting that I knew what was going on otherwise you would not ask."

Now I was confused. I hesitated unsure of how to continue. How would an innocent man react to this question? Would he deny it quickly? Would he object strongly? Would he treat the question with contempt and refuse to answer such an insult? I had shown indignation. How would my interrogator react to this? Was indignation a good sign? Were they asking me offensive questions in an attempt to trap me?

I was to find out later that the interview was being watched through one way glass by a psychologist. Following the interview he assured the detectives that I was innocent. My behaviour and reaction to questioning indicated that. Apparently I was not calm enough and in control to be guilty. He was correct on both counts.

Barclay looked expectantly at me. He appeared to be losing his patience.

"Well?"

In my wild thoughts and utter indignation I had forgotten the question. Or perhaps my brain had simply rejected it as bearing no credibility. Perhaps it was the selective hearing Jane had so often accused me of in the past. In truth I had heard clearly what he had asked but was daring him to repeat it.

"Well what?"

"Did you know anything about this?"

I banged the table in anger.

"No!"

Inspector Jones had been silent so far but now leant forward to speak with affected confidentiality.

"You need to keep calm Sir. This is a serious situation. We do need to ask these questions. You must appreciate our position. We have to think about the safety of your children. If you had any knowledge that would make you complicit."

A ridiculous notion crossed my mind. Were they playing good cop bad cop? Was that slight smile of the face of Jones patronising? Were the pursed lips of Barclay an unspoken challenge? My sensitivities were rampant to the point where I had little control over my reactions.

"How do you know I am not lying?"

He raised one corner of his mouth as if considering his reply and his eyes very subtly flicked to the mirror to the side of us. I only found out the significance of this gesture later when the presence of the watching psychologist was revealed. At that precise moment I mistakenly I presumed it was a look of vanity, watching himself in the mirror. How could he be so callous?

"We will make a judgement on that sir. But you would be best advised to tell us the truth."

Of course he was right, so I relented.

"No I know absolutely nothing about this. I am still to be convinced it is true."

"We are gathering the evidence as we speak sir. But I'm afraid it is already pretty clear. We've had your address under surveillance for some time."

"Don't you need my permission or some sort of warrant?"

Jones shook his head slowly.

"Its standard procedure."

I had a million questions but was struggling to seek some sort of clarity of thought to be able to frame even one. In the chaos something did stand out: the credibility of Jane actually doing what they were suggesting. She rarely ever used a computer and certainly had little understanding of them.

"You say my wife was posting child pornography. I don't understand how she could have done it. She understands very little about technology and the Internet. I even have to show her how to print things. Besides, I am pretty smart IT wise and have put all the protection possible on the Internet. I check on everything that goes on for security. I would have found something."

"Have you heard of the Dark Net sir?"

"Yes. It's an alternative Internet used by criminals."

"We believe that this is what she used."

"But my wife is computer illiterate. How could she have found out about the Dark Net? How could she have understood how to connect to it?"

"It's not difficult sir. There are plenty of low life around willing to show you if you know where to look. Social media is crawling with them."

"Well, I don't know where to look."

"That is probably because you have not tried. Most people find out via social networks. There are people prowling these looking for soft touches. They stay anonymous. They hide behind Internet cafes and public WiFi. These are where the scum play. They are difficult to trace but not impossible. They persuade their gullible victims to contact them via the Dark Net. They show them how to do this."

Anger was focusing my chaotic thoughts. It translated to action as I sat upright and shouted. The ferocity of my outburst shocked me.

"Are you calling my wife scum?"

Barclay sat back in his chair, surprised by my aggression.

"I am simply explaining the real world sir."

It became clear that Barclay was following a check list as he asked a number of simple questions. Most were concerned with my whereabouts at particular times when specific offences were committed. It seems they could pinpoint precisely when certain significant things were posted on-line. I knew that recently introduced powers allowed the police to spy on Internet usage. Ostensibly these powers were to detect terrorist activity but they could be used for almost anything since formal permission was not required. In the light of this my earlier challenge about their activities seemed naïve.

For each occasion I could account for my whereabouts. Nearly all were whilst I was at work and there were any number of people who could collaborate this. Satisfied with my answers Jones closed the notepad he had been scribbling on.

"We will need to talk with your children. We would like you to sit in with them if that is alright with you."

I presumed this not to be a gesture of contrition but compliance with the legal requirement for an appropriate adult to be present. But I took comfort in the fact it showed they were no longer suspecting me. If they thought me guilty they would surely not allow me to be with the children.

"Will my wife also be present?"

"We do not think that is appropriate at this moment. She will be questioned separately."

To my surprise I felt a sense of relief. I did not want Jane to be there. If she had some hold over the children they would clam up. By now my initial shock and disbelief had passed and I was desperate to know the truth. I wanted to hear what the children had to say but wished I could have asked them in private instead of this uncomfortably public place. How could I hold such a delicate conversation in front of strangers?

As they left the room a strange sense of sarcasm arose in me. I silently wished them luck talking to Jane. It would almost certainly be a fruitless exercise. In an instant my feelings changed to loathing as reality set in.

~ 15 ~

In yet another dingy room I sat with Tom. In the far corner a young policewoman stood. She had smiled awkwardly as we had entered but said nothing. Her only action was a casual wave indicating we should sit down. I presumed she was acting under orders. She did nothing to make us feeling comfortable.

Tom sat characteristically swinging his legs under his chair. The thoughts buzzing round in his head manifested themselves in such activity. He was a restless soul and even sitting was expending energy. I sat on the chair next to him and his inquisitive face looked up at me. There was obviously a question on his mind but the strange environment was restraining him. Finally he could contain himself no more.

"Where is Mummy?"

For once he had not referred to Jane as weird Mummy. Had the strain of our situation affected him? I lean closer to him adding an air of confidentiality to my reply. We were sharing a secret.

"Mummy is talking with some men. She will be coming home with us soon."

How could I tell such a brazen lie? It reminded me of the lies I had told when Jane was lying in a coma in hospital. I got away with it then, could I get away with it again? I had no idea when Jane was coming home or even if she was coming home. In fact at that moment in time I knew very little about anything. A tsunami had overwhelmed me and I was drowning. I longed to wake up and find that the nightmare was over. The very real and awake voice of detective Barclay told the lie to this longing. He had entered the room and sat opposite. An awkward smile was fixed on his lips.

"Now Tom, I need you to answer some questions for me."

Tom sat up with keen interest. He was being interrogated just like on the television. His legs swung even harder as he looked excitedly at Barclay.

"OK, shoot."

An even broader smile appeared on Barclay's lips but there was still an awkwardness about it. Perhaps he was more accustomed to dealing with criminals than an excitable little boy.

"I understand you have had some pictures taken?"

"Yes. Lots. Angela and I had to play and do things."

"These things you did, who told you to do them?"

Without hesitation he replied with enthusiasm.

"Mummy told us it was a special game."

"What exactly was the game?"

"Well....we had to take our clothes off while Mummy took some pictures. She said we would become famous. You know, like those people on television. It was just like when I take all my clothes off before going to bed only Mummy had a camera."

I buried my head in my hands. I knew something was wrong but had ignored my fears. The children had been acting very strangely, secretive and conspiratorial. They spoke very little and had lost interest in their favourite toys. They had both seemed to have grown older quickly and were less child like. They were also a lot closer and the arguments that had been so frequent between them had all but ceased. I had assumed nothing more sinister than Jane's behaviour was worrying them. A shared concern had bought them closer. But the conspiratorial nature of their intimate conversations was something new. They spoke in more hushed tones and tended to clam up when I was near. Angela avoided looking at me but Tom would smile innocently. Life was still full of wonder for him.

I despised myself for my blindness and ignorance. I was supposed to be looking after the welfare of the children. How could I have been so remiss? I was so tied up with worry about Jane that I missed what should have been so obvious. I had completely misread the change in the children. How those damned social workers would be so pleased they were right.

I shook my head in despair. What was the point in torturing myself? I was just a normal person and what was happening was beyond normal comprehension. Surely it would have required someone with abnormal perception to see what was going on? And would that person themselves not be suspect? What sort of perverted mind could conjure up such things? Certainly not mine.

As I wallowed in doubt and pity the questioning of Tom continued. How often had Mummy asked him to do it? When did they do it? Did Mummy threaten him with anything horrible if he did not do it? Did she offer him a special treat? A picture was building forming damning evidence of abuse over several months. Piece by piece Jane's character was being torn apart. The case against her mounted from the lips of an innocent small boy.

As I listened my self chastisement for my blind ignorance deepened. I thought I had been caring for my family but the ugly truth told a lie to this. There must have been signs, how could I have missed them?

I realised that this sordid activity must have been done whilst I was at work. Was this why Tom was always so keen to see me when I came home? I had assumed that his waiting and watching at the window for me to calm down was simple childish enthusiasm to meet his father. A couple of times he had not even waited for the angry bear to calm down, rushing out to the car to greet me. He had been eager to risk the angry bear.

There now seemed to be a more sinister explanation. Perhaps my return meant he was freed from the perversion Jane was enacting. Being with me was a safer option than this terrible woman who had once been his mother.

Throughout the questioning Tom continued to swing his legs under the chair and looked his usual cheerful and excited self. Perhaps he had really seen it all as a game. He certainly seemed to be treating the questioning as a game. I held fast to the hope that perhaps there would be no long term damage to his personality or emotional development. Once more I was clutching at straws looking for any sign of hope and a positive outcome. I had little choice in the face of such adversity. If you are drowning then you cling on to anything that might be a life saver however tenuous.

After ten minutes and about twenty questions the police had heard enough. Tom had simply confirmed what they already suspected. As Tom was led away by the friendly policewoman I braced myself for the interview with Angela. This would undoubtedly be much harder and more shocking. Angela was much older than Tom and more easily impressed. She had also experienced the dark side of Jane on several occasions. She would almost certainly not have seen Jane's perverted activities as a game but harsh reality. She would probably have acted out of fear. I had failed to protect her. What would she be now thinking of me?

I was kept waiting on my own with my dark thoughts for five minutes until detective Barclay returned.

“A police psychologist has pronounced that Angela is too distressed to answer questions at present so we will not be interviewing her yet.”

It was worrying news that cut me to the deep.

“Too distressed? What do you mean? Can I see her?”

“It's probably best if she stays with the psychologist for now. She is not speaking at present and we need to handle her with great care. The psychologist wants to spend some time with her to encourage her to talk again. We will call you when she is passed fit for questioning. We are releasing your wife pending our investigations. You are both free to go home. In the meantime we have a court order placing your children with a foster family for now."

My face contorted with an expression of the inward pain I felt. It seemed this torment would never end. I was innocent but not allowed to offer the children any comfort. Instead I was to be let loose with this dreadful woman. It was the last thing I wanted at that moment. This woman was depriving me of the company of my children and I was obliged instead to suffer her company. I was innocent but being punished. Where was the justice in that? I rebelled with anger.

"What? How long for?"

"Just a few days while we get to the bottom of things."

"This is ridiculous. My children are perfectly safe with me."

"Of that we have no doubt but our concerns lie with your wife sir not you. We believe she presents a danger to the children. Unless and until we establish otherwise we will not allow them be in her presence. It is only temporary until we have finished our investigations."

I suspected this to be a patronising lie. If their investigations found what they suspected there was no chance of the children being allowed to come home. Should I challenge this or meekly accept it? I lacked the clarity of thought to decide and said nothing. All options were gone and I was stuck on a single course. What little control I had over my life was fast slipping away. Events were the master. I had become a victim unable to save himself.

Outside in the corridor Jane was sitting on the end of a line of five old wooden chairs. Staring absently at the floor in front of her she ignored my approach. Was she still stupidly blaming me? If so, her denial was of grave concern.

"Jane, we have been told we can go home."

Jane looked up and stared coldly at me. It was a look I had become accustomed to but at that moment seemed much colder than usual. Her lack of any emotional display angered me.

"What about them?"

"The children? They are staying here for now. It's just you and I."

Jane's reaction shook me. She seemed relieved as if some great weight had been taken off her. Her demeanour changed and she brightened.

"Good. They only get in the way. Come on then."

She stood up quickly and strode towards the exit. I had not seen her move with such purpose for a long time. What was going on in her mind? Had she sunk so low that she was glad to be rid of the children? Was this why she had abused them? Had she deliberately created the situation where it was impossible for us to be with them? I became aware of a feeling of shame at the terrible thoughts swimming in my head. I despised this woman profoundly.

~ 16 ~

As was becoming my habit I sat staring blankly at the television. I did not care what was on; my mind was elsewhere. What happens now? I was living a nightmare with no sign of waking. I was alone in the house with this woman I did not know. I found myself wishing they had retained her in custody. If it was a choice between Jane or the kids it was simply no contest. Could things get much lower?

My thoughts were distracted by the sound of Jane shuffling around upstairs. What was she doing? I no longer had any idea about anything she did. Her behaviour was as unpredictable as it was destructive. I wanted nothing to do with her but felt compelled to find out what she was up to. A part of me wanted to make sure she was not causing any new chaos.

Walking slowly upstairs I heard Jane in Tom's bedroom.

“What are you doing?”

I saw she was holding Tom's favourite rabbit, or rather the third invocation of it.

"I am getting rid of some of these stupid toys. Those kids really need to grow up."

"Jane, they are children.. Children like to play. It's how they learn."

"Nonsense. Children learn from their parents."

"And what have they learnt from you?"

She was squeezing the rabbit very hard. Her face had adopted a stern somewhat frightening look. Looking at the rabbit and squeezing harder she spoke with a cold angry voice.

"They have learnt that its a tough world out there and they need to stand on their own feet. They have learnt that there are some horrible people out there."

She was blaming everyone else. I was not going to stand for it. She needed to face the truth and not hide behind self delusion.

"No, what they have learnt from you is that they cannot trust adults, even their own mother."

I heard the words come out and cringed. It was a final and damning condemnation of Jane's behaviour so far unspoken but now given voice. I had tried to be patient and supportive. I had not spoken to Jane about her behaviour. Though inside I was screaming with anger I had suppressed my feelings not expressed any criticism. But now I had lost my patience and understanding and spoken out. This really was a living nightmare.

With a dismissive shrug of her shoulders Jane threw Tom's beloved toy on the bed and walked away. I was left with the realisation that we were no longer communicating. I was someone Jane spoke at not with. She never initiated a conversation and only responded when spoken to. She was living in her own world and treating me as someone at best an irritant, at worst of no significance.

I had never really understood depression but what I was feeling then must have been close to it. It was a feeling of hopelessness and helplessness. The future looked bleak. In fact I could not really see any future. Is this what depression was like? I looked at Tom's rabbit and managed to pull myself back to some form of reason. I had to keep a sense of proportion and reality for the sake of the children. If they had lost their mother they were not going to lose their father.

I picked up Tom's rabbit and gently brushed it back into shape. Despite being the third invocation it was looking battered far beyond the aging treatment I had given it. Tom had been showering it with more affection than usual and it was showing the price. But of course a child's imagination looks beyond this. It sees what it wants to see. A battered toy is a friend. It has life and personality. Tom loved this battered creature despite all its faults. Was this a lesson for me in how I should treat Jane? She was a battered creature with many faults. Should I love her despite this? In that moment it was a challenge I was unable to face.

I wondered if Jane was actually jealous of the affection Tom held for the toy. Had she isolated the children so much that they preferred the company of stuffed toy animals? As I placed the rabbit back on the bed I heard Jane shut herself in the spare bedroom no doubt to be with her private and disturbing thoughts. At that moment I vowed that it could not continue. I had to do something. I could not allow this slide into a dark abyss. We needed help, but what? I did not want to involve any more so called professionals. They were already controlling our lives and were having a detrimental effect. The more they got involved the less I felt in control. Piece by piece they were taking my life away from me. To them we were simply another case to be worked. This mess needed something more intimate and personal.

By coincidence Jane's sister Sarah rang later that day. Sarah lived some distance from us and we rarely saw her. She and Jane kept in touch but only infrequently and of late they had not spoken. Jane had made it clear she no longer wanted to talk to her. At first Sarah accepted the situation. They had fallen out in the past and after a time all was forgiven. In fact they would laugh at how foolish they were.

It was different now. Stories of what had happened had trickled down the family grapevine and Sarah wanted to find out the truth. As I related the whole sorry sequence of events Sarah remained silent. It was unusual for a woman who was normally so talkative. Despite or physical separation I could sense the shock she was feeling.

When I had finished Sarah suggested she could come and visit. I was past being able to reason whether any action would have a positive effect on Jane but Sarah seemed keen so I agreed. She would drive down early the following morning and arrive some time before midday.

Jane greeted Sarah with a detachment that surprised us both. It was as if she were greeting a stranger; someone she had never met before. I recognised the reaction as the same one she had displayed in the hospital in Kenya when she viewed both myself and the children as strangers. To all intents and purposes Jane was looking at a stranger. She certainly made it clear that Sarah's presence was an unwelcome nuisance. But Sarah persisted and they talked for two hours in the dining room.

As I was watching the news for a distraction I could hear the occasional voice. Both sounded calm and neither sounded agitated or annoyed. It was impossible to tell whether things were going well. I was glad at least that they were talking. Jane was not sulking in silence as was her custom these days. In truth she said more to Sarah than she had to me for several weeks. I felt oddly jealous. If Jane had spoken to me rather than ignoring me could we have worked through our problems?

Eventually I heard the characteristic tramp of Jane's heavy tread on the stairs. She used to tread lightly but now walking seemed an effort. Her physical decline had continued. She was returning to her isolation in the spare bedroom. Entering the dining room I saw Sarah sitting with her head in her hands staring at the floor.

"Are you all right Sarah?"

Still sitting motionless and continuing to stare at the floor she slowly shook her head.

"I have no idea who this woman is."

Taking a deep breath she looked up with tears in her eyes.

"She is not my sister."

I could think of nothing to say to such a damning remark. If Sarah did not recognise Jane what hope was there for the rest of us? I stood in silence for several seconds whilst Sarah continued to stare at the floor slowly shaking her head and sighing deeply. I wondered if their past contained something significant. I had read that someone could suppress some childhood trauma that later came out in adulthood.

"Did anything ever happen when Jane was a child?"

"Like what?"

"Something that upset or scared her. Something she might have blocked out of her mind that perhaps has now come to the surface."

"Nothing springs to mind. We had a sort of nothing childhood really. It was boringly normal. I remember we talked about it. We longed for something exciting to happen but nothing ever did."

"Was there ever a time in the past that she behaved strangely?"

"Not that I can recall. She was always the level headed sensible one. It was me that was always getting into trouble. In fact at one time I almost hated Jane. Our parents were always putting her up as an example of how I should behave. She was always Miss Goody Two Shoes."

"That must have been difficult."

"I grew out of it. We all mature eventually and of course I realised that Jane was just being herself; it was me that was the one misbehaving. But that is what is strange. The Jane you see now seems completely immature, like some child out of control. It's almost as if she needs to learn how to behave again. Children are naughty but they are just that: naughty. Jane's behaviour is something more. It's, I don't know, wrong. Its cold and calculating. Its scary."

Taking several slow breaths Sarah raised her eyes to stare at the wall opposite. It was as if that was all the energy she could summons.

"I have a friend who is a priest. Well actually he is my priest but we have become friends. I could ask him to talk to her to see if he can help."

"A priest? Jane is not particularly religious. Was she in the past?"

"No. Not really. But the priest really understands people. He studied psychology before he turned to the church. And he knows about...."

There was something on Sarah's mind that she was reluctant to express, but it seemed significant so I was eager to hear.

"He knows about what?"

"Let's just see what he has to say."

Perhaps a few seconds reflection had changed Sarah's thoughts. I would like to have known what she was thinking but decided to exercise discretion and not push her. If she was reluctant to speak it was not for me to bully her. She was clearly upset and may have said something she later regretted.

Sarah and I spent the rest of the day talking. I was keen to hear all the minutiae of their childhood together. I was desperately seeking something that had happened that would start to explain Jane's behaviour. There was nothing. As Sarah had suggested, they had both led normal unexciting childhoods in the care of loving parents. They had had spats as you would expect between siblings but nothing traumatic. Obviously I was only hearing Sarah's recollection of events, but I knew her to be plain speaking. She talked a lot but everything was strictly factual. The simple events of life were enough to interest her.

Jane never left the confines of the spare bedroom. Sarah took her tea and food but did not stay. It was almost as if she was feeding a prisoner. Departing early that evening Sarah said she would get the priest to call and organise a visit. I was left to contemplate what appeared to be the failure of my desperate attempt to understand what was happening to Jane. Even her sister did not recognise her.

~ 17 ~

I had never taken a particularly philosophical approach to life. It was what is was. I could try to change it but there always seemed to be bigger things conspiring to dictate how I lived. Perhaps I could put up more of a fight but I knew I would probably lose. Such a negative thought did not stand me well in the struggle. As they say, it was a question of picking the right battles. With limited reserves of energy it was important not to waste any on hopeless fights. Life dragged me along and I just tinkered with the odd thing I did not like.

Of course I had choices but the options from which I could select were not of my own making; they were dictated for me. How much choice do we really have if we do not define the options? The one we prefer may not be on the list. Sometimes the choices were plentiful and attractive but all too often it was a question of picking the best of a bad bunch. How frequently did I get that wrong? I struggled to refine my selection criteria but in vain. If I went with my instinct then an unquiet voice nagged me until I changed my mind.

I could do nothing about that damn insect bite. True it was my fault we were in the situation where it happened. I had made the choice on behalf of all of us. But how could I possibly have predicted that? It is not possible to speculate on all the outcomes of everything we do. And if it were possible we would probably end up doing nothing. You could postulate a nasty outcome to everything. All the unpleasant possibilities would be too worrying to contemplate.

Most of the time for me life just happened and I did my best to cope with it. At this particular moment I felt like a lost soul being tossed about in an ocean with an endless horizon. I had no idea where I was, no idea where I was going and things kept battering me. There also appeared to be no chance of a rescue in sight. Options seemed to have vanished and I was on one distinct and uncontrollable course. A dark horizon beckoned and I was marching towards it. I could not stop the march. Something else was controlling my legs.

One thing I would say in my defence is that I never had the desire to turn back time. What happened happened. I was always ready to put things behind me and move on. It was this attitude that was dragging me through our present crisis. I was convinced that better times would come, though at this precise moment that conviction was growing weaker.

I mulled over Sarah's suggestion of the priest. These people did not live in the real world. What would he know about our problems? Though I employed rudimentary psychology in my job I was never completely convinced of its value. To my mind the priest was a man who did not live in my world and practised something I was unsure about. Was it really a good idea? Desperation robs us of reason. There it was again. I was clutching at straws. But helplessness sees us clutching at straws however questionable. Sarah trusted this man and I had no reason to question her judgement. There seemed only one response to this option so I agreed.

They say we form an impression of someone in less that five seconds and that this impression is permanent whatever follows. When the priest arrived on our doorstep I opened the door to see a man in his late forties, slim with the pale complexion of someone who spends all of his time indoors out of the sunlight. His smile was warm and reassuring displaying calm confidence. He had all the necessary attributes to create a good first impression. He had cultivated the art of putting people at ease in an instant. It was probably essential in his line of work.

Appearances suggested he was a man at peace with himself and the world. Some small part of me resented this. Why should he be so lucky when my world was in chaos? I desperately fought the inclination to take a dislike to him.

He introduced himself as Father Lucas as I showed him into the front room and bid him sit down. He politely refused my offer of a something to drink. This added to my feeling of uncertainty. In business it was considered bad form and unfriendly to refuse the offer of tea or coffee. I had drunk countless cups of coffee I did not want simply to show acceptance and avoid the client feeling rejected. In my world it was the first step in a bargain. Refusing the offer set the wrong tone and prejudiced the discussion from the start. Common sense told me I was overreacting. I dismissed the thought as the priest started to speak.

"Tell me about Jane."

"Tell you about Jane now or Jane as she was?"

"It's up to you. I would like to know both in time but for now tell me whatever you want to say."

I paused thinking long and hard. I was not convinced that talking about the old Jane was relevant. I wanted to understand this creature Jane had turned into. The priest smiled seeming to understand my dilemma.

"It's alright Andrew. I appreciate it is difficult. Take your time. We cannot rush these things."

The abstract term 'these things' worried me. It sounded too clinical. Again I was struggling not to resent the calm of this man. My mind was in fight and flight mode. I had become accustomed to dealing with chaos and panic. Even this apparently calm man seemed to be a threat.

Slowly and as methodically as I was able I tried to describe Jane's behaviour rather than her character. In truth I had no explanation for her character. It was completely alien to me. All the while the priest paid uninterrupted attention, nodding occasionally and making an odd sound that seemed to imply he understood what I was saying. He proved to be an extraordinarily good listener. Perhaps this came with his job. I realised that of course, he would have had to listen to many confessions.

Cynically I thought that he had perfected the art of appearing to be interested and attentive. Whatever the truth he inspired confidence and I held nothing back. It was the first time I had unburdened the awful truth to anyone including myself. It made shocking hearing even to me who had lived through it. I started to feel an odd sympathy for myself. This poor man was going through so much. I was starting to detach myself from the awful situation and see things in a different light. My rudimentary understanding of psychology told me this was a form of denial. This was not happening to me but some other poor wretch.

I had expected Father Lucas to ask questions but he simply listened. I heard myself talking in abstract terms about Jane as if relating a story about some fictional character. Was I starting to detach myself from her? As I continued I became distant from what I was saying. It certainly did not feel that I was talking about someone I knew but telling the shocking tale of a stranger.

When I had finished or rather decided to stop unburdening myself on this stranger we sat in silence for several minutes. I presumed the priest was collecting his thoughts. With a deep breath he looked me in the eyes and gave a slight smile.

"Mmm...you certainly seem to have gone through the mill Andrew. I agree that we should have concerns about the children. I have seen cases where the parents have destroyed the lives of innocents."

"The children are my responsibility. I will take care of them. Do you have any thoughts on what you have heard about Jane?"

"I do but first I need to spend some time with her to get to know her."

He noticed the strained look on my face.

"Please don't misunderstand. Its not that I do not believe you. But I would like to form my own impression first hand. We all see things differently and you are emotionally too close. She will behave in one way to you and probably a different way to me. I hope she will not see me as a threat and will be open with me."

"I'm sorry to say she is more likely to react badly to you as a stranger. As I said earlier she does not seem able to cope with anything new. I have wondered whether she is actually suffering from some form of autism. You represent change and that is disturbing."

Slowly the priest nodded his head in agreement.

"Perhaps, but the key with autism is not to appear to be a threat. Somehow you need to blend seamlessly into the moment. If they see you as a natural continuation of where they are then it is not disturbing."

"Do you think you can do that?"

"I'm not saying its easy but I am willing to try if you agree."

I looked long and hard at the priest. Was he talking psychobabble or did he know what he was doing? Only time would tell. I was desperate; anything was worth a try even psychobabble.

~ 18 ~

To my surprise when I went upstairs and suggested Jane came down to meet the priest she agreed. I had expected to be ignored or at best a battle with staunch objections. Perhaps she was curious to see who Sarah confided in. Sarah had talked to Jane some time ago about the man who was her confessor. I recall that Jane had been upset that her sister no longer confided in her but instead preferred the counsel of a stranger. It was one the the things they fell out over. It seemed to her that their sisterly bond had been broken and their relationship was never quite the same again. A distance had formed between them and their lives had started to part. For this she blamed the priest.

Jane walked calmly downstairs and into the lounge. She looked fiercely at me. Her meaning was clear and sensing her resentment at my presence I left them alone. Jane sat in the armchair opposite the Priest and looked at him intently. It was if she were trying to look inside him, trying to read his thoughts. What was he doing here? What was he thinking? Could she trust him? How could this wretched man have come between her and her sister? His calm confident voice broke the silence and interrupted her thoughts.

"Its nice to meet you Jane."

"Maybe, what do you want?"

"A plain speaker eh? That's good. Small talk can be so..."

"Small?"

A slightly strained smile appeared on the face of the priest. In only six harshly spoken words she had made him feel uncomfortable. In a matter of only a few seconds the priest had been given a stark view of the problem.

"Precisely. Sarah tells me that you are not very happy with life at the moment."

"Sarah talks too much. What right has she to talk about me to a stranger?"

"I am not a stranger to Sarah, she is part of my congregation, but I understand your discomfort. She only has your best interests at heart."

"So she says. What do you want?"

"Would you like to talk about how you are feeling?"

"Not really. Its none of your business. Has that man been saying something to you?"

"Do you mean Peter, your husband? He is worried about you."

"He needn't bother. And neither need you."

It was a rebuff that could have ended the meeting there and then but the priest was patient and determined. He was used to dealing with people under pressure and distressed. In such a state people were usually reluctant to speak. Too often they could not clarify their thoughts sufficiently. But for the priest it was effectively the only time people spoke to him. He was also astute and realised that there was no point taking things slowly. His acute perception told him that Jane was a controlling person. She felt most comfortable when things were going as she wanted. He needed to get straight to the point and try to catch Jane off guard.

"Your children are a couple of live wires aren't they?"

"Huh, too much like live wires. They need to learn a little dignity."

"Children certainly can be tiring."

"How would you know? You are not allowed to have children. Though if what we read in the papers is anything to go by who knows? You priests get up to all sorts of things you should not."

It was a personal attack. Instinctively the priest knew he had to interrupt this deflection. He had not come to talk about himself or the church.

"I agree, the church has had rather a bad press in the past few years. But a few rotten apples don't mean we are all bad. But your children, how do you feel about them?"

Jane shrugged her shoulders and uttered a dismissing reply.

"Noisy."

"Yes, they do tend to be don't they? If only we had a fraction of their energy. Life gets so much harder as we grow older. I don't know where all our energy goes."

"Why are you wasting my time with this inane chatter? Get to the point. What do you want?"

"Of course."

Father Lucas stared into Jane's eyes. They were cold and tinged with anger. They were the eyes of a truly disturbed woman.

"Are you finding that your illness is tiring you so much that the children are a little difficult to cope with?"

Again the dismissing shrug of her shoulders served as a reply. She spoke no words and gave the priest a withering look. Once more he looked into her eyes and saw them change taking on a colder darker appearance. She scowled menacingly and a mocking smile appeared on her lips. Her voice took on a lower and harsher tone.

"You are asking me questions. Now its my turn. Do you believe we have always had caring instincts?"

It was an odd question that momentarily unbalanced the priest.

"I am sure yes. Just look at wild animals. They have an instinct to protect their young."

"Yes but eventually they turn their back on their young. They see them as rivals. They kick them out. Some even eat their young when times are hard."

"Perhaps the analogy is too tenuous. Animals are not people."

Again Jane smiled cruelly, mocking the priest.

"But people are animals. Its only behaviour that makes us different."

"There is much more to it than that. I believe there is something inside us that makes us different from animals."

Again the mocking smile from Jane.

"I suppose its a God given gift."

It was not a question but a statement filled with cynicism. She continued in the same vane.

"At what point in human evolution did we develop a conscience?"

Uncomfortable as the conversation was getting the priest continued.

"I am not sure what you mean."

"Well, early human beings were savages. They killed each other mercilessly. They even ate each other. It was perfectly logical. If food was in short supply then why waste good protein? People lived together in small family groups but at some point they started to live together in larger groups. So when did they develop a conscience to care about others? People have developed a collective culture of right and wrong. But how do you know it is right? What if millions of years and billions of people have got it wrong? What if they have been self deluding all this time?"

"That is unlikely. Have you heard of the concept of the intelligence of the masses?"

"Of course but its a myth. Errors proliferate other errors. Once an error is made it leads to others and they multiply. Look at cancer. One cell goes wrong and it multiplies until it leads to the death of the host. Is that logical? Why would a cancer kill the host that it lives in? It is illogical self destruction. It makes it impossible to reproduce. It does not make sense to care for others above yourself. What is the point in existing? Only yourself matters. The human race survives because individuals survive. Surely you've heard of the survival of the fittest? Why should I care about the survival of the weak?"

At this point the priest realised he needed to choose his words carefully. The woman in front of him was lucid and eloquent but to his mind not thinking like a normal person.

"But should we not sacrifice ourselves to ensure our children survive? They are the future not us."

Jane waved a hand to dismiss the comment with contempt.

"Who really cares about the future? Why care about it when we will not be here to see it? That's illogical. Aren't we all concerned about the here and now? You asked me how I feel about my children? I created them I want back the life I gave them."

Shocked the priest pulled an anxious face.

"That is an odd thing to say."

Jane lowered her voice and spoke to the wall opposite avoiding the uncomfortably intense gaze of the priest.

"When I created them they took something from me. I want it back."

"What do you think they took from you?"

"My integrity as a person. They have my genes. I have no control over what they do with them. They also took part of my mind."

"I don't follow. What do you mean part of your mind?"

"I am less of a person now."

"But children add to our lives. They enrich us."

Jane now turned to the priest with anger in her voice.

"That's nonsense. They simply drain the life out of us. They take and give nothing back. Your life is set on a course and then children come and wreck it. I hate them."

As uncomfortable as the conversation was the priest determined to dig deeper into the mind of this disturbed woman. However sinister her thoughts they were clear and she believed them.

"How do you see your husband Andrew?"

"He's a weakling. He smells of weakness. I despise him. My life was perfect until he came along."

"Really? You don't think that he added something to your life, a partner, a friend, someone who supports you through thick and thin? Look what he is doing for you now."

"More nonsense. I would be happier if he went away. In fact I would be happier if he did not exist at all. Him and his pathetic children are of no use to me. I wish they were dead. It's like my sister. She's too weak to talk to me herself so she sends a monkey along."

"But surely she spoke to you yesterday."

"Some wretch of a woman spoke to me but it was not my sister."

"You are talking about the people who love you and care for you."

"Do they? What they care about is that I become a subservient slave who acts the way they want and says what they want me to say. That's not caring."

Breathing slowly as he tried to clarify his thoughts the priest spoke in as caring a voice as he could muster. There was a subject he wanted to raise but was struggling. He decide to use the trap of asking a reasonable question that would be unreasonable to refuse.

"Can I ask you a question Jane?"

"You can ask what you like. Its my choice as to whether I answer."

"Of course."

Uncertain the priest frowned and looked hard at Jane. Suddenly realising the silence Jane turned to confront him.

"Well?

"Why do you self harm?"

Jane's face lit up and a smile formed on her lips.

"Have you noticed what a spectacular colour blood is?"

Again the priest looked hard at her. Was she deliberately trying to shock him? She had certainly avoided answering the question. Smiling even more broadly Jane tried to add to his discomfort.

"Life hangs by a thread doesn't it? Its fascinating how you can see your life dripping away with every drop. Then you put your finger on to stop it and it stops; the body recovers. Life goes on. We have so much control over life and death."

"But life is precious. It cannot just be thrown away."

Jane's face took on a more sinister look. She was suddenly becoming angry.

"Who are you to tell others what they can and cannot do?"

"You seem very angry Jane."

Jane shrugged her shoulders. What did she care what this man thought?

"You are meddling in affairs that are nothing to do with you. You are on the wrong side."

"Wrong side? I do not understand."

Jane looked at the priest with loathing.

"We are not interested in your sanctimonious self righteous claptrap. It would be better if you leave us now."

It was not really a suggestion but an order. Jane turned her back on the priest and fell silent. Questions crossed the priest's mind but he realised it would be futile to voice them. In truth he was also worried about the answers they would receive. He had done as Sarah had asked. It was time to leave.

~ 19 ~

Jane and Father Lucas spoke for over an hour. This was more than Jane had spoken for weeks. She did not hold conversations. When she spoke to me she used very few words and made it clear it was a one way conversation and that I was to listen. She was not interested in anything I had to say and usually ignored any question. Even the simple offer of a drink was ignored as if unheard. If she wanted a drink she made it herself without bothering to ask me. At times she made me feel less than human. She certainly made me feel that I meant nothing to her. Any hint of a sign of recognition was accompanied by anger and irritation.

I was desperate to know what had happened during such a long conversation and was displaying the sort of enthusiastic eagerness I saw so often in Tom. With considerable effort I managed to restrain myself as the Priest settled down in the arm chair opposite. He spoke calmly and thoughtfully, considering every word carefully.

"In a conventional sense Jane is perfectly sane. She speaks clearly and logically. Her thoughts are well reasoned. In fact it is difficult to argue against her logic even if it is alarming. But it was very odd. At times I thought I was talking to someone else. It was as if she was relaying the words that someone else was speaking. In truth she is..."

Father Lucas became silent. Whatever was on his mind was troubling him deeply. I recall Sarah had started to say something similar but she also stopped short of speaking her thoughts. What were these two thinking? I resented the withholding of his thoughts and spoke with an unfamiliar and forceful emphasis. It was a paradox that I did not completely trust this man but wanted to know what he was thinking.

"She is what?"

Staring intently at the ground the priest spoke quietly.

"I am not sure how to put it without offending you. She has a dark soul."

"A dark soul? What does that mean?"

Taking several long and slow breaths the priest looked me in the eyes and spoke in a quiet voice almost whispering.

"We all have a dark inner self, I call it a darkness of nature. Our whole lives are a battle to keep it under control. Jane has surrendered to it. In surrendering it has taken over."

I rejected the hammer blow. He was being ridiculous.

"That makes no sense."

Slowly he shook his head and continued in his near whispering voice.

"On the contrary, it makes perfect sense. Her behaviour is rational according to what she believes. It is only our perspective that makes her look unusual. To her she sees nothing wrong in her behaviour. She made a valid point. As a society we have a consensus on right and wrong but who is to say that is valid? Can we really say that someone who behaves differently is wrong? Values change. What was once seen as right can become wrong and vice versa. Who is to say that what Jane believes now will not be acceptable at some point in the future?"

"If you will pardon my saying, that is philosophical bull shit. There is clearly something seriously wrong with her mind. What I want to know is what we can do about it?"

"It really needs someone who can relate to her as she is now. Someone who has a similar moral compass. Our inability to get past what we see as her inhuman behaviour will always act as a barrier to understanding. It needs someone who is already the other side of that barrier."

"Is there such a person?"

"I have come across many. They are lost souls who live in a different world to us. It's as if they have crossed some forbidden divide and gone to a new world. But it's a terrible world with little humanity. These people have become less than human which is why we struggle to understand and relate to them. The paradox therefore is that such a person would not care to help someone else."

"Do you mean people like mass murderers?"

"That's a little extreme but possibly. Such people commit murder without any thought or feeling for the victim. They see no wrong in what they do. They have lost the ability to behave as rational human beings."

"But we call them insane not murderers as if its not their fault. We ascribe some illness to their behaviour. We lock them up in special institutions. Do you really think that is where Jane belongs? Do you think Jane's behaviour is her fault?"

Pausing the priest collected his thoughts before continuing.

"That is an impossible question to answer. If we act in ways we believe to be right are we at fault? If our belief system is wrong is it our fault? If we cannot recognise that what we believe is wrong we cannot change it. Is it more or less honest to follow what you believe? Or should you go against what you know is right because someone else does not approve?"

"So how could one of these people help?"

"It needs to be someone who has been to the other side but returned."

"Returned? How could they have returned if they have no way of knowing what they do is wrong?"

"You see the paradox but some people do return. We don't really understand why. I believe there is good and evil in all of us and that they are always in conflict. Even an evil person has a sense of right and wrong. It may be very different from our understanding but it is there. However evil someone is there is always good inside them somewhere struggling to come out. It nags away at the evil sometimes gaining small victories. Perhaps the good will eventually win. It may not be the same good that we understand but it is better than the evil."

My mind was rejecting what I was hearing. We were not having a cosy discussion about life and the universe. This was my wife we were talking about. This was the motehr of two small children who now despised and neglected them.

"I am struggling to understand what you are saying. Can I ask you something? It might seem a little odd"

For most of our conversation the priest stared at the carpet in front of him. His meeting with Jane had clearly disturbed him. With a rapid jerk of his head the priest looked up.

"Of course."

"Do you think she is possessed?"

"Do you mean demonic possession? I can see why you might think that but I don't actually believe in it. Well, it's not quite as black and white as that. I believe that the devil is in us all of the time. We just need to keep him under control. When we don't and he shows himself in our actions, it can seem like we are possessed."

"That's a little evasive."

"It is not my intention to be evasive, just to answer as sincerely as I can. One thing I have learnt in my years as a priest is that the more I learn about people the more I realise I do not really understand them. Each scrap of knowledge merely serves to show me there is so much more to know. Its as if each new scrap of knowledge is just showing me a pathway to more knowledge. But the path is long and without end."

Intentional or not this evasion was not helping me to understand what was happening to Jane. Had anything come out of his talk that gave us a better idea?

"So tell me what she said."

"You must realise that a conversation with a priest is confidential."

"But surely normal conventional ethics do not apply in a case where, as you say yourself, the person is not normal? Beside which it was not a confession in the accepted sense."

"You are wrong. Of course they apply, perhaps even more so. It is important to gain trust and that cannot be gained if confidences are betrayed. Jane seems to be harbouring a lot of anger and contempt towards you. If I am to help he she must be confident I am not telling you anything about or conversation. She will pour the same contempt on me and clam up."

I shook my head displaying a large degree of the contempt I was feeling.

"That is all too convenient for you isn't it? It epitomises the reasons I distrust your kind."

"I'm sorry you feel that way. I realise you are under a lot of stress..."

I was getting increasingly angry and interrupted.

"Don't patronise me. It was not my idea for you to come."

Though I was starting to resent this man with his calm and knowing manner I wanted to know more.

"Why does she look at things as if they were new? In hospital she did not recognise me or the children. She seems to have forgotten almost everything about her life."

"I think you are wrong. You told me earlier that the virus damaged her brain but it does not seem to have affected her memory. She remembers almost everything. Only it seems that she does not like what she remembers. Its as if she is looking at a person she once was and hates them. Your wife is a strange paradox, I believe she is struggling to cope with her new self. The demon is free but there is still some part of her that is fighting. But that part is scared of what it sees. As I say, its a paradox."

This was a strange notion that needed time to sink in.

"You think there is nothing wrong with her memory?"

"Yes. But as I said she does not like what she remembers."

"She told me once that in her dreams she sees a dark figure beckoning her towards him. What do you think that means?"

"One possibility is that its her innermost self calling her to be someone else."

"You don't seem very sure."

"When it comes to the mind we can only speculate. Oh, we think we are wise and can see into people's heads but its more guesswork than science. We once thought the insane to be possessed then we rejected the notion. We believed it was the same mind only it was ill. Now we incline to believe something between the two. There is a school of thought that now believes in possession only we are possessed by a dark self inside us."

This constant use of the term 'we' was starting to annoy me. Was it a cheap trick to try to add credibility to everything he said? It was not his opinion and open to question, it was collective and therefore more credible. Or was it a means of distancing himself from something in case it was wrong? I was beginning to wonder which one of us was the psychologist.

Rising to his feet the priest looked at the wall opposite again avoiding eye contact. He sighed deeply.

"I have probably overstayed my welcome."

I wanted to stop him and talk more but resisted the urge. The conversation was difficult and disturbing and I needed time to consider what he had said. With a handshake noticeably less enthusiastic than the earlier greeting the priest bid me good-bye and left.

I ruminated over what had just transpired. Had I been too quick to dismiss his thoughts? As a civilised society we have a generally accepted view of what is evil and what constitutes an evil person. Surely Jane did not fit this view? She was not committing mass genocide. She was not exploiting the misery of others for her own gain. To my flailing mind she did not tick any of the boxes that qualified the description. But I could not take a dispassionate view. However great a distance Jane was placing between us I still felt an emotional tie.

I paused as the events of yesterday came flooding back. Jane was being investigated for child pornography. She was exploiting the misery of our children. Was the priest right? I played through the many things that had happened in the past weeks. Was Jane indeed behaving as an evil person? I continued to dismiss the thought as ridiculous. What did this man know sitting in his ivory tower in his closeted world?

To my mind his talk of possession and dark souls sounded like the plot of a film.

~ 20 ~

Following the visit of Father Lucas things developed at an alarming pace. Once again I felt that some unstoppable force was in control of our lives, dragging us in directions we did not want to go. Any protest or resistance was futile. Our once calm and measured existence was being bullied beyond our control and I could do nothing to stop it.

Recently introduced special new powers enabled the police to retain suspects in prison if they believed them to be a danger to the public. The government had reacted swiftly to a series of high profile cases and public clamber for action. A desperate, struggling government duly obliged even though Brussels disapproved. They craved the publicity of seeming to be strong and acting purposefully but panic had tainted their perspective.

Under these draconian measures Jane was incarcerated pending her court case. The police believed they had gathered enough solid evidence to prosecute her and secure a conviction. With this certainty and their conviction she was guilty they deemed her a threat to the public.

Though the compassionate side of me rebelled against such an extreme measure I fought to suppress this reaction. Whatever was driving our destiny I surrendered to its latest twist since there was a plus side. It meant the children were free to come and live with me. It pained me to acknowledge that I had sunk to new depths. I actually welcomed the fact that Jane was to be locked up.

Though I was glad to have the children back I also felt a selfish satisfaction. It was a move that finally showed that I was not under suspicion. We could try to get back to some sort of normality. With the police convinced of their case I could start planning the future again with some certainty. It would be a future without Jane at least for the short term and for however long she was sentenced. Long term perhaps it would be even better. With a jail sentence for such an awful crime behind her I was convinced Jane would be deemed an unsuitable parent. A glimmer of hope had entered our insane world. I was off the hook. I had been relieved of my lingering duty of care for this woman.

This comparatively period of quiet also gave me a welcome chance to engage a solicitor and discuss what options I had whatever happened to Jane. As a first step the solicitor applied for an order that prevented Jane from seeing the children. I did not fully appreciate the need until he pointed out that without such an order I could be obliged to take the children to visit Jane. At that point she had not been found guilty and retained certain rights however perverse. It would seem that again I was not in control and could not decide what was best for them. Some faceless bureaucrat would make the decision. This continued obsession with the belief that children were always better off with their mother was tough to fight.

During a call from the solicitor he told me that Jane reacted very badly when she heard the news of my application. Due process dictated that she must be informed to give her a chnace to contest it. Certainly I was subjected to a tirade of angry abuse when I next visited her. She became so agitated that she had to be restrained and taken away from the visiting room. I had expected Jane to tell me not to come back but she clearly retained enough sense to realise that severing all connection with me would be a mistake.

It was uncomfortable to hear but the solicitor assured me that this violent behaviour harmed her case and helped mine. Sure enough, within a week he had secured the court order preventing Jane from seeing the children. It disturbed me deeply. I still harboured the remote possibility that Jane might recover and was acutely aware that withholding the children could reduce this possibility. They were an integral part of the old life with the old Jane we all longed to see again. I had crossed a boundary. I was now prepared to do things that could harm Jane. Though certain I was doing the right thing it sat uncomfortably with me. I no longer held to the oath I had made in sickness and health.

It is difficult to find anyone beyond the liberal chattering classes who believes that our Human Rights legislation makes sense and represents true justice. Possibly the only exceptions are the lawyers who make more than a comfortable living fighting the often unworthy causes. To many people such as me the legislation appears to offer more support to the wrong doers than the rest of us. It is certainly the perpetrators of criminal acts that make most use of it. We meantime are obliged to tolerate the situation where in effect we fund the guilty in their appeals. We have no choice. There is no opt out clause. I have no power to say that I do not want these people treated so softly.

I had always maintained the opinion that if you commit a crime you are opting out of human rights. If you take yourself outside of the law you should take your chances. You have opted out of the protection of reasonable people. Human rights are the rights of law abiding people. Rights are earned by appropriate behaviour; they should not be assumed. So it was with some dismay and anger that I heard from the prison authorities that Jane had secured a lawyer to argue her case for access to the children. I had a court order granting me permission not to take the children to see her. She had harmed them enough and it was now my duty to protect them. Jane was now seeking to overturn this. Why was she being so bloody minded?

Jane's lawyer was arguing that since Jane had not yet been found guilty her rights were being infringed if she was kept away from the children. When I received a call from the prison administrator telling me she had received instructions to allow visits I screamed down the phone:

'What about the human rights of my children?'

Of course the response was polite but reaffirming the ridiculous position. The argument was sickeningly clear. In the absence of any conviction I could not prevent Jane seeing the children. My original court order had been throw out.

I was about to rant at the caller but common sense told me it was not her fault. I was shooting the messenger. She may even have agreed with me but could not show it. She too was another innocent victim of ridiculous legislation. There are so many of us.

After a long and tortuous conversation with my solicitor I was forced into the inevitable. Yes I could fight it but it would be expensive and of more concern the children would get dragged into it. They would almost certainly be questioned to see what they thought and how they felt. Cynical lawyers would play us off against each other. They would almost certainly try to paint me as a bad parent. They would do everything to justify their thirty pieces of silver. I had to decide which of two bad options was best for the children.

In this way Jane would still be hurting the children. It was even possible that Jane would be granted permission to see the children whilst the case was in progress. I gave in without a fight though my hatred for Jane grew stronger. On many occasions she had made it clear she despised the children. What was she up to? Was she trying to get back at me? Was she still in denial? Did she still hold me responsible for everything? Was she using the children to exact some sort of perverse revenge on me? If so for what? What had I done wrong?

As a safeguard my solicitor had insisted that all visits were supervised by an accompanying social worker. My presence was deemed insufficient since Jane had displayed a hostile reaction to me. If she did this again it could harm the children. Somehow Jane was still turning this back on me. It was my fault she would react badly and the children would be harmed. Justice was pointing at me as the culprit. And the lawyers grew fatter.

Initially I objected but quickly accepted that it was in everyone's interests including mine that all interaction was monitored. My solicitor believed that if Jane took even the slightest step out of line we could appeal and get the order overturned. An independent view was essential to the success of this. Apparently my opinion was worthless. This only served to reinforce my view that I had been let down and betrayed by the law.

The first meeting was difficult and fraught with tension. In truth the children did not want to be there and I found myself in the profoundly hypocritical position of having to persuade them. Even from the first meeting Jane came across as friendly and warm, nothing like the creature we had seen recently. Was it an act or had she changed?

For a fleeting moment I hoped that the old Jane was coming back to us. But there was something in her manner that discomforted me. As she interacted with the children she seemed to be studying them intensely. Then there were the furtive glances at me to see if I was watching. When our eyes met a hint of disapproval briefly crossed her face. She resented my presence or more probably the inhibiting effect it was having on the children. Whenever Jane said something slightly odd they would look round at me as if seeking guidance. All I could do was smile uncomfortably and show insincere support.

After a few visits it became clear to me that underneath the apparently friendly exterior Jane was cold and calculating. To me her behaviour and every action had some hidden intention. When I mentioned this to the social worker assigned to accompany the visits she adopted a somewhat intolerant and patronising voice. Without actually using the term she politely suggested that I was being paranoid. Even my solicitor questioned whether I was giving it enough of a chance or deliberately trying to be obstructive. In my own mind I was convinced something was wrong. I was living high on emotional energy and very sensitive to everything going on. I was desperately worried about the children. This woman that was once my loving and caring wife could not be trusted.

During the supervised meetings Jane and Angela often sat together chatting. Oddly they had seemed to have grown closer. My mind was in a complete state of doubt and confusion. Was this good or bad? Would Angela's comparative innocence have the effect of bringing Jane back to reality, or would Jane's perverse and frightening behaviour rub off on Angela? I felt powerless to do anything. Whenever I went near them they would clam up. Angela seemed quite happy to sit with her mother. I was being excluded.

Jane's glances at me had changed. Now she seemed less disapproving more content. I longed for this to be a good sign but all my reserves of hope had been depleted. All that was left was my anger and suspicion. I remained convinced she was up to something. I was sure she was preying on Angela's naivety. To my eyes Jane's look of contentment seemed to contain a hint of smugness. Was she wallowing in her victory over me? She certainly no longer saw me as a threat. Even in the confines of a prison she could win over me. This did not bode well for the future and my attempt to keep her away from the children.

~ 21 ~

One of the duties Jane had abdicated even before her arrest was the dreaded and almost universally despised school run. Normally quiet roads become chaotic accidents waiting to happen. Those who get caught in the chaos are angry and frustrated. Even the mothers who perpetuate the chaos seem to hate it and tempers flare regularly. What should have been a pleasure sharing an activity with their children was quite the opposite. It was an activity filled with annoyance and resentment. It was an interruption to whatever other activities they had planned for the day. Technology had made them free. School time was their leisure time. Even shopping could be accomplished by the click of a few boxes on a computer screen. The school run chained them again. It was an attack on their freedom. They are latter day martyrs surrendering their lives for their children.

As a child I had always walked to school but today's children cannot raise the energy. The need to ferry children by car is rationalised with arguments around safety. Are children really less safe walking the street today than when I was a child? If they are surely there is a better answer than cramming the roads with cars driven by fraught parents? It is the school run itself that presents a danger on the roads. When children walked to school the roads were much safer.

And then we are told there is an obesity epidemic. Children need more exercise and a walk to school and back would seem to be a logical solution. Instead of getting some vital exercise the children sit in the back of the vehicles in stately calm sending texts or watching DVDs whilst their highly stressed chauffeurs rage and shout at the other traffic. Don't these mothers realise what a poor example they are showing their offspring? Is there any wonder so many children have little control over their behaviour? Why should they exercise self restraint when their mothers do not?

Perhaps these parents ferry their children as a substitute for affection. If that is the case it was not working. Many of the children I encountered were most certainly not very loveable. Quick tempered and demanding they were precise copies of their parents.

Though the daily warfare on the road with mothers who were little better than unpaid taxi drivers was infuriating the waiting at the school gates was far more uncomfortable. I would stand as the only father waiting. I was conscious of eyes watching me and a host of unspoken questions. At least, they were unspoken to me.

Paranoia is a strange an uncomfortable condition. It is the brunt of many jokes but is most certainly not funny to the sufferer for whom there are demons around every corner. If you believe people are talking about you how do you know who is and who is not? If someone is looking at you are they talking about you, or are they simply looking in your direction? We all soft focus, absent-mindedly looking at nothing. We have to look somewhere. Usually we look at the person we are talking to but there is a limit. If we look too much we are staring and make the listener feel uncomfortable. So our eyes tend to wander and will land without attention on other things.

Psychology teaches us that where we look whilst talking gives away what we are thinking. Irrespective of what we are saying our eyes are giving visual clues to what is really in our minds. That person looking at you may be displaying a characteristic visual clue or you may just happen to be in the way. In a state of paranoia it is impossible to decide. All clues lead to the same conclusion.

As I stood waiting for Angela I appeared to be in a lot of people's sight. Were they looking at me or simply letting their eyes wander? I had to admit I did stand out. Amidst an exclusive female gathering I was the only man. I probably looked awkward as I fidgeted uncomfortably. Did they think I was some sort of pervert? There were often stories in the news about men hanging round school gates. It was also the province of drug dealers waiting to prey on the naive. I was new and unfamiliar, perhaps I was a drug dealing pervert.

I was immensely relieved when I could take Tom with me. It showed that I was innocuous and harmless. I was further relieved when Angela appeared and I could demonstrate to the watching eyes that my presence was completely innocent. What I had not bargained for was the fact that so many of the waiting women knew of Angela's situation. Putting two and two together they quickly deduced that I was her father. As the days went by their curious looks transformed to disgust. I really did have a reason to feel paranoid. They were indeed looking at me, loathing me and feeling superior. With the sparsest of knowledge they had found me guilty.

I had learnt a defensive technique to help me cope with difficult work situations. I would imagine the other person as being themselves the object of derision. I would conjure up some reason to look down on them. This diminished their threat and gave me confidence to stand up to them. In practice this was not difficult with most of my colleagues. So much of their behaviour was open to derision. I rarely had to invent a reason not to like them.

I felt defensive under the gaze of these women and compelled to practice my technique to repel them. How did I know that some of these women were not looking at pornography themselves? It was perfectly possible that they were supporting these on-line evil groups. Someone supported these groups, why not these women? They had plenty of free time whilst their children were at school. Perhaps it filled a void in their humdrum lives. How did I know some of these women were not secret drug takers? Perhaps they felt the need to take drugs to relieve the stress of the school run.

Weren't one in four women on tranquillisers? How did I know some of these women were not child molesters who beat their children?

I would stand and survey each woman in turn trying to assess whether they looked like the sort of person who would be so deviant. I half closed my eyes frowning and gave each a long hard deliberate stare. At first they seemed to talk more, probably commenting on this strange man who kept staring at them. But after a couple of days the tactic worked perfectly because some started to look away when our eyes met. They seemed to be embarrassed. Perhaps I was right. Perhaps they had guilty secrets they were afraid I knew about. It is incredible how much power the unspoken word has and how much a look can disarm.

In a perverse way I began to enjoy these meetings. Guilt and suspicion can be seen everywhere if you looked hard enough. After all who could possibly have guessed that such evil could happen in our apparently normal family? As I by now knew too well, closed doors can hide a multitude of sins.

Mercifully Angela was being spared adverse attention from her school friends. She had certainly made no complaints and the headmistress of the school was not aware of any problems. Perhaps Angela too had learnt a defence mechanism. Or had moral standards degenerated so much that the children did not care? Could they not even be bothered to rise to the depravity of bullying? Perhaps Angela's situation even fascinated them and made her an object of interest. She was different; she was special. Much as I would have liked to dismiss this last thought it lingered. I did not want Angela to revel in her situation.

There was a lot of talk about kids sending compromising pictures of themselves via mobile phones and the Internet. Was such behaviour becoming accepted as normal? How could nine and ten year olds lose their innocence without any objections? How could we surrender moral standards without a fight? Children were our future but what corrupt and degenerate future would we be living in if this continued? Things that some of my generation perhaps only thought fleetingly and dismissed were now being acted out. What damage would this do to immature minds?

My gradual victory in the silent battle with the mothers seemed to change their attitude towards me. Some started to acknowledge me with a greeting and the physical distance they had previously maintained began to shrink. Eventually we stood close enough to engage in conversation. At first it was innocuous chatter about the children and the odd things they did. But slowly they started to express our mutual concerns about the dangers they faced.

Once they had plucked up the courage to talk about my situation they started to show me some sympathy. It seemed that many were afraid that the nightmare I was facing, or something similar, could easily happen to them. Was this the reason they all drove their children to school? Were they anxious to spend as much time with their children in the hope of keeping them from harm? If so they were under an illusion. As I knew, children can be exposed to danger in what should be the safety of their own home.

As I came to terms with the stress of the school run it represented an unexpected but welcome return to normality. It was what normal people did. Now that the women no longer mistrusted me it represented an activity of comparative calm. I even started to take some pleasure in it. I must have been the only one that actually enjoyed the school run. Had my life come to this sorry state?

~ 22 ~

After a surprisingly brief court case Jane was found guilty of peddling child pornography. Throughout Jane had said virtually nothing and remained impassive in the dock. At times it seemed like she was elsewhere. Her eyes would glaze over with that fixed stare I had grown so used to. It was as if she were lost in her own thoughts unaware of what was going on around her. Whatever was going on in her head bore no connection to events in the real world.

Amidst overwhelming evidence Jane steadfastly refused to defend herself. It was almost as if she wanted to be found guilty. I wondered if perhaps she took some pride in what she had done and wanted the public acknowledgement. Or had her lawyer persuaded that her best chance was to try to show diminished responsibility? Were they conspiring for some sort of mental illness plea? Events were making me suspiciously cynical and I was starting to misread many things.

With the current clampdown and publicity surrounding child pornography the judge had no alternative but to give her a custodial sentence. She was to be incarcerated for five years. The judge also ordered a review on her release to determine whether she should be excluded from approaching myself and the children. Hearing this pronouncement was the only time Jane reacted throughout the whole case. She snarled alarmingly at the judge and muttered a string of oaths.

Prior to the case this would have seemed an extreme sentence. As the harsh reality of what she had done was revealed in court it turned out she had been indulging in a number of other activities with various groups that were being monitored by the police. Some of these groups were associated with child trafficking and child slave labour. Disgusting child images was bad enough but these revelations came as a profound shock.

Somehow Jane had become entangled in a network of criminal activity. There had been some flow of money and it was this that obliged the judge to come down so harshly. Pictures were one thing but child trade and exploitation were viewed as far more serious. The public wanted action and results.

As I listened to the damning evidence it all started to make sense. I should have asked myself why Jane had suddenly become so flush with money but there was too much else to concern me. Our financial situation had always been open and clear but Jane had started to have a private financial life. She had opened an on-line bank account. The occasional ring on the front door heralded the arrival of a courier bringing something else Jane had bought on-line.

I had convinced myself that this activity was a sign of Jane returning to normality. She had always enjoyed retail therapy but after our last experience I did not dare risk another expedition.

My longing had made me blind. I had been stupidly naïve. By being obsessed with trying to come to terms with everything I had failed to notice any new developments. Being unable to reconcile past events had blinded me to what was happening in the present. I struggled to cope with the behaviour of this stranger as she seemed to be building a new life for herself.

Believing Jane had already reached a low point I had not noticed her sinking even deeper. She had bought a new computer claiming her old one was too slow. I supported this as it seemed to be something she was interested in. Everyone kept telling me that I had to support and encourage any signs of her returning to normality. I kept my paternal eye on the new computer but had failed to detect what she was doing. It never crossed my mind to delve that deeply. It never crossed my mind she could be so perverted. When it came to using computers it was the children I was concerned about not my wife. She was supposed to be a responsible adult. In a foolish moment I blamed myself for allowing her to degenerate into this world of filth. But is passed.

It was several weeks before I was allowed to visit Jane in prison. They had conceded to her mental condition and she underwent therapy. It was explained that my presence might interfere with this. Apparently the first few weeks were critical for prisoners to come to terms with their situation and visitors were not allowed during this period. This period of adjustment was thought to be especially difficult for Jane given her mental state.

But it was not just me that was excluded. Her crimes meant she was held in isolation away from other prisoners. It made sense for her but it also made sense for me as it gave me time to come to terms with what had happened, or at least find some form of accommodation. Finding sense would take a long time if it were even possible. Had it not been for this cooling off period I would probably not have visited anyway; I was too upset and angry. The hatred I was trying to suppress had grown.

After my third visit it was becoming clear that incarceration was having a profound effect on Jane. Her eyes were fierce and blazing with anger. Being held in isolation for her own protection seemed to be reinforcing her lack of reality. She needed people to be able to keep a hold on reality but it was too dangerous for her to be with the other inmates.

Perversely even the hardest of criminals hated any offences against children. For many of these women the only thing they saw wrong with their criminal act was being caught. Crime was an accepted way of life and in their world crime was socially acceptable. They even took pride in what they saw as their achievements. But in this deluded world some crimes were not acceptable. They viewed paedophiles as less than human and deserving of any punishment they could mete out. A mother who could exploit her own children was seen as beneath contempt. There was no lower form of life. It deserved any punishment they could mete out.

It was a perverted view but strongly, even violently held. To them it was justice and the perceived injustice of their own incarceration only added to the ferocity of this view. There was in effect another justice system within the prison, one administered by the prisoners themselves. Whenever they got the opportunity they administered their justice with pleasure and a clear conscience. They lived in a world alien to me. It was a frightening world with incomprehensible morals. It was if they were an alien race.

The prison staff also bore some hostility towards child offenders but on the whole continued to carry out their work professionally. Jane learnt quickly that they were strict and tolerated no nonsense. Even amongst the officers there was a strange sense of justice. A woman who abused her own children was despised as a life form lower than other prisoners. Such life forms were tolerated but with great reluctance. Rules of conduct that governed the behaviour of prison officers were often ignored when they dealt with such prisoners.

I was to learn however that one woman warder had developed some sympathy towards Jane. As a trained psychologist she had been assigned to Jane as the first step in her rehabilitation. I found out later that they had spoken often and Jane had started to convince her that there was some doubt about her guilt. On my visits she would take me aside and tell me as much as she could about Jane, her health, her mood and what she was talking about. I tried to seem interested but it was a difficult pretence to maintain. I was fast losing any sympathy towards her. I really did not care what happened to Jane day to day and as for what she was thinking I cared even less. It had been a long time since anything Jane said made sense to me.

Jane had persuaded the warder that it was all Angela's fault and that she had taken the blame to protect our daughter. She spun the lie that it was Angela that posted the pictures that had been taken in all innocence. Jane's lies were given credibility by an increasing number of stories appearing in the news of children behaving this way. They were posting questionable pictures of themselves on social media. It was almost as if there was a competition to see who could post the most shocking picture. So profuse was the activity it had acquired a name: sexting.

This fabricated web of lies had enabled Jane and the warder to form a loose bond of friendship. Though this was generally discouraged in the prison they seemed to have made an exception for Jane. It kept her calm and quiet and came to be part of her rehabilitation.

At first I was unsure as to how to react. It was likely that if I tried to correct the delusion by reiterating the truth Jane would condemn me to the warder. She would certainly portray me as a bad father and possibly even complicit in the lies she had concocted about Angela's behaviour. Who would the warder believe? I could not risk being accused by Jane. It was imperative that I stayed above suspicion for the sake of the children. I dare not risk Jane's filth tainting me. Social services continued to lurk in the background watching.

As I tried to wrestle with the dilemma I became concerned that I was beginning to understand how Jane thought. How could I possibly understand the mind of someone so evil? What did that make me? Hadn't the priest told me that it would take someone evil to understand Jane?

Even before her incarceration Jane had developed an immensely strong character. This gained even more strength in prison. It was not an attractive character, quite the opposite, but there was no denying the strength of it. It seemed to me that Jane was increasingly able to control the new personality she had become. And with that she was able to exercise control over people around her. She had truly become a different person from the woman I married. I did not recognise her and I was starting to fear her.

The almost wild animal she had turned into had gradually become tamed and with her new found confidence and self control she was becoming manipulative. She revelled in attention and increasingly craved the company of others. But I could see this craving had an ulterior motive. She wanted to get into people's minds to probe and disturb. She tried it with me several times but everything that had happened acted as a block to any relationship. I was not going to let her get close. I needed to act as a barrier between her and the children.

I only visited because I felt obliged to. It was a sense of duty rather than any lingering affection. It was impossible for me to tell whether Jane either welcomed my visits or resented them. We spoke very little and over time my visits grew shorter. The Jane I had loved no longer existed. What was there to talk about with this stranger? I wanted to end the misery of my time with her.

I felt at times like a social worker assigned to a prisoner to give them contact with the outside world. Often I contemplated suggesting the authorities find a qualified and willing visitor to take my place. I was made aware there were such organisations. But some nagging part of my conscience held me back. Did I still harbour the hope that the old Jane would return? If so I wanted to be there to comfort her when the shock hit. This Jane still seemed detached from everything but the old Jane would be horrified at what had happened.

~ 23 ~

With Jane having been found guilty I assumed that I would now be able to stop her seeing the children. To my intense anger my solicitor cast some doubt on this. He believed we would have to re-apply for the rescinded court order granting me a ban. Apparently once an order had been overturned it could not be re-activated. Possible changes in circumstances rendered it invalid.

It would also be necessary to apply to have Jane's order overturned. It was another example of the madness of our legal system caring more about the protection of the perpetrator rather than the victim. It was also supporting the legal gravy train that kept solicitors and barristers well fed.

Without doubt, and again at our expense Jane's lawyer would counter with the same lie about her human rights. But my solicitor seemed confident she would lose this time. She had been found guilty of a crime against the children so finally the law would be obliged to protect them. A mother may have considerable rights over her children but not to do them harm. Jane had demonstrated her willingness to do harm in brutal fashion. As long as I stayed out of trouble and above suspicion I would be granted absolute custody. As legal guardian my wishes for their welfare would be paramount. If I did not want her to see the children my wish would be respected.

It sounded odd to be called their legal guardian but the law required clarity. Father I may be but the law was more interested in my suitability as an appropriate adult. So much had changed in our lives which were now being governed by legal requirements rather than the need for the children to have a loving family. I sometimes felt I was surplus to requirements. I was left with the impression that I could be replaced by someone else deemed suitable. Parental rights seemed to be taking second place. Understanding the legal logic did not settle my fear of the uncertainty.

Following my solicitor's advice I stopped taking the children immediately. On further advice I ignored the letters I received from Jane's solicitor. They were suggesting that I was not complying with the court order and threatened action against me to make me comply. Again the solicitor confirmed that the court order obtained by Jane was no longer valid. They were playing a sick game.

I also ignored the letters because in principle my solicitor wanted to force their hand and hoped they would give up. He believed them to be a bluff in the hope I would submit to their bullying. Unfortunately a singular characteristic of Jane's new personality was tenacity and she demanded they pursued their case. When something entered her head nothing would shake it. Her tenacity and venom seemed particularly acute where I was involved. Did she really care about the children or simply want to win a victory over me?

Again I pondered over this new Jane. The Jane I knew would not have been so stubborn. She would have cared foremost about the children. She would have compromised for their sake. Now she seemed to be trying to exploit them. But exploitation was the reason she was in prison.

I desperately wanted to stop all contact between Jane and the children permanently and determined to do whatever was necessary. My fears for the harmful effect on them had been confirmed. It was noticeable that they had changed as a result of the visits. They had become even quieter and less communicative. Even Tom had started to calm down and had lost some of his childish sparkle. Angela seemed to have adopted a permanent scowl, the soft lines of her young face becoming harder. It was as if her mind was deep in thought over something that troubled her. I tried to talk to her but she dismissed my approaches. She made me feel like I was interfering and being a nuisance. We were beginning to drift apart.

It was a new experience for me to be brushed aside in this way by one of the children. Angela was now close to being a teenager and all teenagers rebelled seeing their parents as interfering. But this was different, something more profound. There was mistrust in her eyes. To my deep distress I saw that she looked at me in a way I had seen Jane look. Was I too late?

I had grown to distrust the telephone. It kept bringing bad news. Business was tough in a difficult economic climate. Even at work the calls seemed to be bad news. Nothing could have prepared me for the day Sarah called me at the office.

Three days a week Sarah came and looked after the children. Her collecting them from school was a blessing as it avoided my brush with the mothers and the school run. Though I had come to an accommodation with them things had worsened since Jane's conviction. I had hoped they would show some sympathy but instead they displayed contempt. It was as if they blamed me for letting it happen. I could see the unspoken questions in their heads. How did I not know what she as doing? And if I did, why didn't I stop it? Wasn't I just as guilty?

When I heard Sarah's voice I feared the worse. She was in a state of panic and her stuttering was only vaguely comprehensible. What she was saying struck me a paralysing blow.

“Angela is dead. I found her dead. She's taken pills, lots of pills. From the bathroom cabinet. Some of the anti depressants Jane was on.”

I could summon no words and sat in silence. I hoped I was asleep having a bad dream or that my imagination had become so perverted it was making up what I was hearing. Sarah's pleading voice rang in my ears.

“Andrew?”

“I'll come home straight away.”

To the surprise of my colleagues I dropped the phone and hurried out of the office. I recall nothing of the actual drive home; my mind was too full of noise.

Hastily parking the car I tore up the garden path and fumbled my key into the lock on the front door. Inside the house was crowded. I recognised the social worker who I had hoped never to see again but there were three other strangers.

I grabbed Sarah's arm in panic.

"Where's Tom?"

"Its alright. He's next door with your neighbour."

As I stood bemused by the chaos Sarah hastily pointed out who these strangers were. Two casually dressed men were police. The smartly dressed man scribbling on a note pad was the doctor called by the police.

When Sarah had tried to get hold of me I was in another interminable and pointless meeting. In my absence she had called the police. It seemed sensible though I deeply resented the intrusion. I had had enough of people interfering in our lives. Had I not spent months convincing the police and social services that the children were safe with me? How would they resist saying: I told you so? Suspicion was bound to fall on me. Questions would be asked. What had I done to drive Angela to this? Hadn't I stopped her from seeing her mother?

At the prompting of one of the policemen everyone gathered in the front room. With a detached coldness that angered me the doctor gave his prognosis. The fact that Angela had simply fallen asleep and would have felt no pain was of no comfort. Did he mean that or was it patronising nonsense meant to reassure me?

If I was shocked and angered by what the doctor said the story from one of the police detectives was more horrifying and more shocking. It defied rational and human belief. They had been investigating the activities of a man called Robert. At least this was the name he used on-line. They believed it was him that had persuaded Angela to enter into a suicide pact with another girl. Angela had been chatting on-line with this man for some time and the interaction was being monitored.

When the call came through from Sarah they picked it up and came immediately. He seemed genuinely sorry for being too late and not acting earlier but the evidence they had put together was sketchy and insubstantial. They were powerless to act without more solid information. So much of their work was thwarted by having to wait for something to happen. They investigated crime rather than preventing it.

My mind rebelled at what I was being told. I was angry, angry at the police for being so slow, angry at Jane for her continued evil effect on our lives and angry at this Robert. Through the rage a revelation struck. Surely this was not the same Robert Angela had said was Jane's friend? If so Jane had introduced them. Had Angela been chatting on line with this Robert for months? I had been remiss once before not picking up Jane's criminal activities. Was I remiss for a second time? Why did I feel it was my fault?

Time passed quickly as I sat in silence with my thoughts. One by one the invaders left the house, the doctor, the welfare worker and one of the detectives. Only a policewoman remained waiting for the arrival of a van to take Angela away to the mortuary. Finally I watched as they carried her tiny body out of the house. Only Sarah and I remained, not speaking and unable to look at each other. In the ashes of this unimaginable tragedy, what was there to say?

I passed the next two days in a haze. Moments of clarity were interspersed with blank nothingness. I had turned into myself seeking answers to questions I could not understand. How do you cope with the suicide of one of your children? We are supposed to protect our children. I had failed as a parent in the most ultimate of ways. What should I have done differently?

Tom was behaving as if nothing had happened. The police woman who attended the house on that dreadful day had the presence of mind to grab Tom and whisk him away before he knew what was going on. To him it was just another adventure. The police were back. Could he have his fingerprints taken again?

We told him Angela had gone away and he seemed happy with the explanation for her absence. As Angela had spent more and more time in her room on her computer they had grown apart. She had lost much of her capacity for looking after her younger sibling. At times when Tom pestered her she would snap at him. I dismissed her behaviour as a consequence of growing up. All young girls of her age have moods don't they? Weren't they struggling with hormonal changes? The last thing they needed as they explored the world was a little brother being a nuisance.

Tom had taken to amusing himself. He did not seem to need company. I should have been concerned about his lack of friends but rationalised the concern away. I told myself it was difficult for him given our circumstances. He would make friends once things had settled down. I could reason almost anything away but not the loss of Angela.

I found out later during a visit to the prison that when the warden who had befriended Jane broke the news to her she was shocked by Jane's reaction. Jane had smiled. It was as if she was not seem surprised by the news. I dismissed this as nonsense. How could Jane possibly have known?

At first the warden put this reaction down to the new drugs Jane was on. She had been particularly restive and violent recently kicking out at everyone and everything. Most of her privileges had been withdrawn following a fight with another prisoner. This had made her mentally unstable. But after the shocking news she had become much calmer and more content. In an odd remark the warden even suggested that the news had been more effective than the drugs.

It was not the reaction the prison authorities had expected. Their latest theory was that her behaviour was due to shock. It was yet another theory in a long line of explanations for Jane's behaviour. In truth they had little understanding of the complex woman. My cynicism told me that they needed to put a label on her behaviour so it could be neatly filed away. I saw nothing to deflect me from this view. They had the unfortunate job of looking after this wretched woman and if they needed to hang a label on her it was understandable. It justified the drugs.

I could not summons the courage to visit Jane for several weeks. Had it not been for the pressing of the authorities I may never have got round to it. I finally succumbed to emotional blackmail. Did I have no compassion? How could I abandon a mother that had lost her daughter under such extreme circumstances? Though I was becoming hardened to my emotions it was difficult to admit this to others so I gave in.

It was a strange visit. Jane seemed more relaxed and outgoing than I had seen for a long time. She did not seem at all distressed. But there was still no warmth in her. She was still cold and unfeeling. She still treated me with contempt. She wanted to know exactly what happened and revelled in every clinical detail. She repeated much of what I said almost delighting in the repetition. I felt uncomfortable and was angry with this repulsive woman but managed to control my temper. It was a point of principle. I did not want the watching guards to think me unable to control myself. There had always been this vague lingering suspicion that Jane's problems were linked to me. Liberal feminism pointed the finger at men.

Though never going so far as to state it directly Jane left me with the feeling that she blamed me for what had happened. Several times she emphasised that as she was in prison she could not protect the children. She pointedly suggested that it was my responsibility and I needed to take more care. She told me she was talking to her solicitor again for the right to see Tom. She did not trust he was safe in my care.

After half an hour I could take no more. I stood, glared angrily at her and left. I wanted to look back but feared what I might see on her face. So low had my opinion of Jane become, I feared I would see a look of smug satisfaction.

As I collected my things in the reception area I was approached by the warder that had befriended Jane. She invited me to join her for a catch up. It was during this conversation that she told me about Jane's odd reaction to the news. She seemed genuinely worried about what she saw as Jane's apparent mental decline. Without doubt Jane had got into her head and played on her emotions.

For an instant I toyed with telling someone of my concerns, but I wanted as little as possible to do with Jane. Expressing my concerns to the warder's superiors would open a can of worms that could only cause me further grief. I wanted as little as possible to do with Jane.

~ 24 ~

Angela's body was being held whilst the police continued their investigation. It was incomprehensible to me as to why they wanted to torture me this way. They knew what had happened. They knew who was to blame. Why weren't they trying to track down this Robert? Why would they not allow me to bury Angela and try to come to terms with my loss?

My anger and frustration had grown beyond all bounds. I never knew I could display such intensity of emotion. It consumed and overwhelmed me. It was almost as if I too had become a different person. In the past I was able to rationalise pretty much anything. I had even managed to rationalise what had happened to Jane until things had gone past the limit of tolerability. But now I floundered and was sinking, unable to think straight. Any rationalising made no sense and was self delusion.

I needed to do something to break out of my introspection. I needed to occupy my mind and allow things to be pushed into the background. I determined to track this Robert down. Enticement to commit suicide is an offence but until we knew who he was it would not be possible to bring him to justice. Finding this low life was a campaign I could lose myself in and I took it on with enthusiasm. This restored some life into me. I had a reason to wake up each day. I was hunting a killer.

My crusade was given impetus by the fact that to my immense frustration the police showed no interest in finding this man. Perhaps they had given up on us. They already had far too many dysfunctional families to deal with. Jane was a convicted child molester. Why should they give us any priority?

Did they really buy the story of Robert? How many disturbed teenage girls took their lives each year. Didn't all grieving parents want someone the blame? If they sat on their hands for a while the case would fade into history, yet another insignificant unsolved crime. No one would be interested. It would become another cold case.

I demanded a meeting with Inspector Vinall and after several angry calls to the station he finally agreed.

At the meeting we talked about Angela's death but my anger grew with what Vinall had to say. He suggested that teenage suicides were not unusual and therefore not something they paid a lot of attention to. It was a blunt response bordering on brutal. It was clear he had neither the time nor patience to justify the behaviour of the police.

He suggested that there were a number of contributing factors: peer pressure, social media, hormonal changes, difficult family circumstances. Anything could play on a fragile and immature teenage mind. He implied it was an obvious and expected consequence. Their files were full of similar incidents.

I was incensed at the suggestion that it was my fault though it was not difficult to see his viewpoint. The last year of Angela's life had been traumatic and largely down to her parents. Between us Jane and I had created the environment in which this could happen. Of course it was mostly Jane's fault but did I do enough to support Angela? Should I have taken more notice of the warning signs? Should I have ignored her brushing me aside and been more firm? I was not a bully but perhaps I should have been. It was all futile hindsight and only made me feel worse. Each dispassionate comment from Vinall stuck the knife in deeper.

Despite my revulsion at his suggestions somehow Inspector Vinall convinced me that I shared some responsibility. But in doing so it gave him an excuse not to care. If it was our fault why would they bother wasting time and resources? We had let Angela use the Internet without proper constraint. It was irresponsible parenting. He was remarkably adept at deflecting blame.

If we had allowed Angela to be exposed to this man Robert then we were culpable. At one point he even used the term, contributory negligence. Though he carefully applied a context to the remark it stood out on its own. It was this that finally caused me to explode and storm out determined to pursue things myself. How did he think it was helping to accuse me of being an irresponsible parent? In my mind the blame lay squarely at this mysterious Robert. He needed to be found and brought to account.

In a final twist of sick irony Vinall warned me against taking the law into my own hands. In a defiant act I stood in the door way and shouted at him.

"Why not? If the police are not prepared to uphold the law then someone else has to. The alternative is anarchy. It seems to me that all you want to do is tick a few boxes and file it away. Well that will not do!"

Without giving him chance to reply I walked off. I realised that this outburst would almost certainly mean they would be keeping an eye on me. With this thought my anger flared to new heights. They did not have the resources to look for an evil man who encouraged my daughter to take her own life but they would find the manpower to keep an eye on me.

For the second time recently I began to experience the distressing feeling of paranoia. I could not reconcile how life kept kicking me but letting the bad people off. This was not how it was supposed to be. I had always believed that there was a natural order of justice but this belief was being torn apart. I had led a good life. I did not expect a reward but I most certainly did not accept the grief that was being thrown at me.

Since Angela had been communicating with Robert via the Internet I decide this was the best place to start hunting for him. My own knowledge of IT was extensive but not sufficiently to enable me carry out the digging necessary to track him down. I needed help and persuaded one of the whizz kids in our own IT department to help me.

William was an absolute fanatic about all things to do with computers and willingly agreed without asking questions. He also readily promised to keep silent about our special exercise. I hid the real purpose of the exercise in a hazy story. I had persuaded him that I wanted to understand just how secure the Internet was. How easy was it to track down someone that was trying to hide? It would make a change from his humdrum work of fixing the mess my fellow employees made of their computers or changing ink cartridges. His excited curiosity at something new and covert secured his agreement. Cautioning me to leave him to it and not to make inquiries lest he be discovered he promised to contact me as soon as he found something.

To use as an example I gave William some of Robert's details I had noted when I had been sorting out a problem on Angela's computer recently. We had come to an agreement on her secret password so my earlier fears for her safety had faded. I did not realise until too late how wrong I was. In hindsight the fact that Angela had stopped caring about whether I found out what she was doing should have been a stark warning. But what parent willingly thinks the worse of their children? Emotional attachemnet means that blindness comes too easily.

Two days later my computer pinged with an instant message. It was from William and contained a simple message: *Cracked it!. Sort of.* I replied suggesting we meet for a coffee in a cafe near the office in an hour.

When I arrived William had already finished one cup and eagerly accepted the offer of another. He frequently joked that real IT people had coffee flowing in their veins. That certainly would explain why they always seemed so hyperactive. It also explained why they always seem to be needing the toilet.

As I placed the coffee in front of him I could no longer contain my eagerness to hear what he had discovered.

"When you say you've cracked it, what do you mean?"

"It's a bit odd."

"Odd how?"

"Well, as best as I can work it out, the origin is either Wormwood Scrubs or Holloway Prison."

"Really?"

"Uh huh. The addresses point to a government network and the domain is the prison service."

"Do prisoners have access to the Internet?"

"Some do. Our company does some work for the prison service maintaining the kit. Isn't one of your sales colleagues responsible for selling to then public sector?"

"Yes, I believe so but its all a bit hush hush. He had to sign the Official Secrets Act."

"Ah Right. Well, using computers and the Internet is part of prisoner rehabilitation training. It puts them back in touch with the real world. There is a prison Intranet, an internal network. A smart prisoner could hack it and connect to the Internet that way. Most prisoners just play games but some do educational courses which require access outside the confines of the prison. Let's just say there are a number of ways it could be done if someone knew what they were doing."

My mind exploded with anger. Prisoners were being enabled to prey on young girls via the Internet in the name of rehabilitation at my expense. What kind of justice was this?

"Don't they screen what the prisoners do?"

"It's quite difficult to monitor everything. And some of the prisoners are very IT smart. There's probably even prisoners inside for computer crime. They reckon that at least twenty five per cent of crime in this country is computer based. Its probably more but the police struggle to keep up with it. They've set up specialist computer crime units to try to cope."

"Why did you come up with two prisons?"

"Educated guess. The origin is the prison service Intranet which is a bit messy to understand but I can keep digging."

"Thanks William. I need to give this some thought. You will keep quiet about what we have been doing?"

"Of course. But if there is anything else I can do let me know."

I hesitated considering the question in my head. William had managed to find out more than I expected.

"Have you in effect hacked the network?"

"Not quite which is why I can't quite figure out the actual origin. Why?"

"Just curious."

William gave me a cynical look.

"If I can be blunt Andrew, I think there is more on your mind than mere curiosity. Do you want me to hack the network? You do appreciate that would be a serious offence: hacking the prison service. I could end up getting an inside view on the network!"

"Of course I would not want you to do anything illegal."

"It's a bit late for that now. Even just sniffing the network is probably a crime."

"Do you mean you have gone beyond what is publicly available from the signatures and addresses?"

An odd conspirator look crossed his face.

"Maybe, but perhaps it would be best if you did not ask. You could be accused of being an accessory."

"I do appreciate it William."

A smile beamed across his face.

"Appreciate what?"

~ 25 ~

Tracking down Robert started to become an obsession. At first I had convinced myself that his discovery was essential for the sake of justice but this idealistic view changed inexorably as the days went by. As the police failed lamentably to make any progress it had turned into a crusade driven by anger and malice. I was not interested in justice but revenge. This despised stranger became the focus of all the pain, frustration and anger I had built up over the past year. It was irrational but I began to blame him for everything.

In the dark hours of night I started to imagine what I would do to him once we had found him. Forget the due process of law. It would be too slow and the punishment handed out would be derisory. We are far too soft in this country. Other countries know better how to deal with the scum that pollute and harm our society. They make them pay. We treat criminals with kid gloves obsessed with their human rights. We offer them false sympathy. Liberal dogma drives current thinking. Its not their fault. They are victims of a disadvantaged upbringing or circumstances. We should support them as they are rehabilitated back into society. And what happens to all this care and attention? It is thrown back in our faces.

Over half of all criminals re-offend. The low life laugh at us and treat us with contempt. They do their worst and we give them a slap. Well I would show this low life he could not get away with it. These people need to be taught a proper lesson, a life changing lesson that is so harsh they will never commit crimes again. I would teach Robert a lesson he would not forget. I wanted an eye for an eye. No, I wanted more than an eye. Equality was a nonsense. You did not restore balance with equality; you had to go further. With right on your side you should tilt the balance more in your favour.

I started to research how I could get hold of a gun. It was a wild thought but something deep inside was compelling me. As my mind twisted and schemed I began to realise that the thought of vengeance was a comfort. In the hell I was living very little provided comfort. Only odd moments when Tom was his old mischievous self were a beacon in the darkness. How could I not smile at the scrapes he got into? If there was the possibility of mischief, he would find it. But in my current frame of mind the thought of another person suffering was providing something to look forward to. It gave my desperate existence purpose.

Though I did not realise it at the time I had lost my sense of reason and perspective. I craved for diversions to occupy my mind. I had even started to enjoy work more. There was a stable sameness about it. It contained no real surprises just the predictable round of politics and back stabbing. Where once these would have angered me now I had something more significant on which to focus my anger. What did I care about the petty scrimping ambition of colleagues? Their struggles to climb the ladder were undignified and laughable. I was beyond all that. My life was not that petty. I became aggressive and self serving and in consequence more successful at my job. I had become like the colleagues I despised. The area sales manager tolerated my bad tempered moods because I was delivering results and his bank balance grew.

William informed me that his search had ground to a halt. He was tip-toeing carefully to avoid detection and this was inhibiting him. It would seem that the police were starting to monitor the prison networks for signs of criminal activity. He was coming close to being detected.

He assured me that the setback was only temporary and that he would win eventually. Whoever this Robert was he seemed to be very smart and capable. He covered his tracks and hid his identity well. We could not contact the police or prison authorities for help since it would have meant owning up to our activities which as William had suggested were almost certainly illegal.

William and I had become conspirators. We could often be seen in the local coffee shop chatting and looking at something William had uncovered. It was surprising just how much access prisoners had to the Internet. They were supposed to be incarcerated to keep them away from society and yet were allowed a lot of access to the outside world. It was supposed to be strictly controlled but William was right, there were some very clever people in prison who had committed computer based crimes. Their knowledge far exceeded that of the authorities who had neither the time or resources to police all prisoner activity properly. Was there also the suspicion that prisoners locked into hours on a computer were quiet and no trouble? I had seen for myself the soporific effect computers had on people. It was as if they were on drugs that suppressed their minds. As William put it: prisoners playing shoot 'em, kill 'em games tended to be more passive.

I was sat at my desk deep in the details of a difficult contract when William approached from behind and tapped me on the shoulder. His voice was quiet and confidential.

"We need to talk."

"OK, coffee shop thirty minutes. I need to get this contract over to our legal people today. You would not believe what this customer is asking for. I think they are on some chemical substance. I need to work out just how much give there is in our offer and see how close it comes to what they are asking. Then I've got to get approval. Customers, they're a pain."

I looked up at William and realised that my idle chatter was not welcome. His face had an expression that told of some great discomfort in his mind. A normally carefree character, I had never seen him look so worried.

"What's wrong?"

"I don't want to talk here. But we do need to talk urgently. I will see you over there."

Thrown by his manner I struggled to concentrate on the contract. In the end I capitulated to most of the unreasonable customers demands and dispatched the contract to the legal team. It was likely it would be thrown back at me but if they came back with questions or objections I would deal with them later. Meeting William was a more pressing need.

In the coffee shop William was sat at our usual table. It was in a position that gave us a degree of privacy and also largely out of sight of the ever present queue at the counter. We did not want anyone from the office to witness our clandestine meetings. With the heightened sensitivity of office politics, people were always suspicious and saw conspiracy in the most innocent of situations. Three people were a meeting but two people were a conspiracy.

As I sat down William was turning an empty cup round in his hands. It was an unusual gesture and in keeping with the air of withdrawal that hung over him. Fear welled up inside me as I realised he must have some bad news. Out of respect I waited patiently for him to speak. His words were harsh and reluctantly spoken.

"I have tracked Robert down. The messages originated from Holloway."

I was confused by this surprising news.

"Holloway, isn't that a female only prison? So is he someone who works there?"

"No, Robert is a prisoner, a woman prisoner. It's a handle, a pseudonym. Its a way of hiding yourself."

"Are you sure she is in Holloway?"

"Yes. All computer usage is recorded. I managed to hack into the records. One of the messages was sent when a particular prisoner was using the computer."

"Do you know who?"

William fell silent starting at the table in front of him. He was still fiddling with the empty coffee cup. It was not like him to be so disturbed. It was not like him to be so silent. He pursed his lips and sighed quietly.

"It was your wife. Robert is an alias she used as part of the ploy to cover her tracks."

I was stunned. It was as if I had been struck a mighty blow on the head. The truth was too shocking to accept. In the silence between us the horrendous conclusion formed in my head: Jane was responsible for Angela's death. All the comfort I had been taking from thoughts of vengeance disappeared in an instant. I would not be allowed the satisfaction of seeing Robert suffer in recompense for his crime.

I was in a panic. What should I do? Should I report what we had found? I could keep William out of it and lay all the blame at my feet. I worked in IT; they would believe me. Surely they would be sympathetic to my distress? But what purpose would it serve?

I did not care about Jane. I now saw her as less than human. I still wanted some sort of revenge but if it became public knowledge what would be the effect on Tom? He still harboured the hope that his mother would come back. Would it be better to let him live with this forlorn hope or know the real truth? Could a five year old cope with such a truth? In fact how was I going to be able to cope with the truth?

The silence that had fallen between us as we kept our own thoughts was disturbed when William stood up. Without a word he left me. In the doorway he looked back and waved but my thoughts were elsewhere in a much darker place. I had never imagined life could be so hideous, so evil. In that moment reality seemed a long way off. My mind was struggling to cope. I longed to wake up somewhere else, anywhere else. I wanted to be in a world without Jane.

~ 26 ~

I had not visited Jane for over a month. I could not face her with the dreadful truth I knew. My mind was still in a state of shock. In truth my visits had been pointless long before this. I did it because I was pressured by the authorities and in particular the psychiatrist in charge of Jane. I hated going, she resented my presence and we would sit not speaking and barely looking at each other. Now I could not possibly look at her. This awful truth William had discovered made the thought of seeing her repulsive in the extreme. I did not trust how I would behave in her presence.

Beyond refusing to visit Jane I was undecided as to what to do about William's dreadful discovery. Things were bad enough without adding something even more horrific. The revelation would only make matters worse. There would be another investigation that would intrude on and disrupt our lives. I would be back in the limelight and Tom would inevitably be involved. It was this that worried me most. If Jane were not stopped would she somehow get through to Tom? The thought filled me with horror as I lay awake wrestling with the seemingly irreconcilable dilemma. Should I speak up and see justice done or keep quiet and spare Tom? Could I protect him? I had failed with Angela.

It was that short period in the early hours of the morning when the Sun was hinting at rising and my room was filled with half light. Shadows were emerging from the background slowly starting to reveal the shapes of familiar objects. It was still quiet with no sound from the sleeping world but something had disturbed me. In a semi-conscious state my brain was not quite awake. Opening my eyes wider I saw a dark figure standing at the foot of the bed. As I stared at him he moved towards me and touched my arm. I shuddered with the coldness of his touch.

I should have been frightened by this stranger in my room but my feelings were more of curiosity. If he had wanted to harm me he would have done so whilst I was still asleep.

"Who are you? What do you want?"

Slowly, almost mechanically he shook his head and spoke in a deep menacing voice.

"I want nothing from you."

His words had been deliberately chosen but unclear to me.

"What do you mean?"

I could not make out his face but he appeared to be looking directly at me. There was an air of anger and irritation about him.

"I already have one of your children. I have come for the other. You are not a worthy parent. You are supposed to protect your children and now one of them is dead. You made your wife into a monster. You were supposed to love and protect her. In fact you are not a worthy person. Tom would be better off with me. He is in danger with you."

My instinct to rebel seemed to have vanished. Instead my mind tried to reason with the dark figure. Some perverse part of my brain saw sense in what he said.

"I have always tried my best. I love my children. I love my wife."

"But one of your children is gone and your wife is no more. She is someone else. She does not love you. And you are lying; you do not love her. Love for you is something you think you must do but in truth you do not know how. I can feel the hate inside you. You hate your wife. You wish she were dead. What sort of father does that make you? Tom would be safer away from you."

I looked hard at the dark shadowy figure. I still could not see his face. Was he taunting me? My instinct to kick out had returned. The dark part of my brain that was reasoning with him had shut down. I cried in anger and desperation.

"Go away, leave me alone! Leave my children alone."

I suddenly awoke to my arm being shaken frantically and the sound of crying. Turning I saw Tom standing by the bed distressed and upset. He was trembling uncontrollably. He spoke with a weak but anxious voice.

"Daddy, why are you shouting? What's wrong? I'm frightened."

Sitting up sharply I grabbed him, lifted him quickly and cuddled him close to me. It was an act of comfort but for whom? I struggled to hold back my tears. I had to be strong.

"Daddy was just having a bad dream. It's OK now. Its all over."

Tom was still sobbing but more quietly. He spoke softly into my chest, his voice uncertain and frail.

"Was it that man?"

"What man?"

"That dark man who comes at night."

My eyes widened with horror. I thought I was alone in this nightmare. I turned Tom to face me and looked deep into his eyes still moist through tears. His face was filled with a sadness I had never seen.

"Tell me about him."

"He talks to me. He wants me to go with him. But you told me never to talk with strange men so I don't. I just hide under the duvet until he's gone. I don't like him. Make him go away. He's, he's..."

Tom sobbed again, lost for words. I felt horror of a depth I had never known before. My mind raced with illogical thoughts. We were having the same dream. How could we have conjured up the same dream? Did some mystical reality lie behind it or had Tom and I come so close our minds were working the same way? Were we thinking the same thoughts and imagining the same things? Had I infected him with my fears and worries?

Again the horror swamped me and flooded my mind with wild thoughts. Had this stranger appeared to me because I was stopping Tom going with him? Was he trying to remove the obstacle to taking Tom? Why did my mind keep asking so many questions? What had happened to my ability to find answers? My thoughts were interrupted by a gentle sob from Tom as he took a deep stuttering breath. He was looking up at me with pleading eyes.

"Does he come very often?"

"Yes. Lots. I don't like it Daddy. Make him to go away."

I stroked his head reassuringly, but who was there to comfort me? Did this figure come from the depths of my soul? But it was more than my dark imaginings; Tom had seen him too. I had read about mass hysteria where many people experience the same emotional stress. Is that what we were suffering? I dismissed the notion. Though we were both on emotional tenterhooks neither of us was behaving hysterically.

It had been a traumatic and damaging few months and we both seemed to be coping. But how did I know if Tom was coping? Perhaps he was clever at hiding his thoughts and feelings. He would certainly have got that from me.

As I tried to make sense of what had happened the thought of the social worker entered my head. I was supposed to report any unusual behaviour by Tom. I could talk about him having nightmares but how could I admit I was having the same dream?

"Tom. We must not tell anyone about this."

"You mean its a secret like Mummy's?"

I was horrified. What was I doing asking Tom to keep secrets? Secrets were why we had got into so much trouble. I dare not play games with his young mind. I needed to keep him in the real world.

"No. Its nothing like Mummy's secrets. Mummy was naughty. In this case the man is being naughty."

"Ah, right. So the police do not need to know about this secret."

As I feared, it was too late. He had already started to learn about lies and deception. In a cowardly act I accepted the situation and agreed with him.

"No. We will sort this bad man out ourselves. We will tell him to leave us alone."

By now the Sun was rising and as we both lay on my bed half sleeping I quickly formed a plan. I decide that from now on Tom would sleep in my room. If this stranger appeared again we would confront him together. I would move his bed in and leave a small night light on. If Tom needed to get up in the night I would go with him. When Tom went to bed I would work in the room across the hall with both doors wide open so I had a clear sight of him at all times. Tom would never be on his own at night again. This stranger might try to scare me but he was not getting anywhere near Tom again. He had chastised me for not protecting my children. I would show him he was wrong.

The following afternoon Tom and I moved his bed or rather I moved his bed and Tom tried his best. In practice he was more of a hindrance but we were doing something together. It was an adventure that excited him and he looked to have forgotten the distress of the previous night. Separating day and night was something children could do. As adults we tended to see everything as one. Each new day brings new adventure to a child but to us adults the past lingers haunting us.

My plan seemed to work. For several days Tom slept soundly and my own sleep was undisturbed by unpleasant dreams. The stranger did not come back. I thought we were safe again until one late afternoon Tom was sitting on the floor of the lounge playing with his latest favourite toy, a large metal truck. He was quietly chanting a riddle over and over.

"Two little ducks, sitting on the water, one had a pee and the other said he oughta."

"Where did you learn that Tom?"

"The man."

"Which man?"

"You know, the one that comes every night. He taught me last night."

~ 27 ~

I know it was insane, completely insane, but after many weeks of the pain fermenting in my head I felt compelled to confront Jane with what we had found out. My revulsion at the thought of being in her presence had now been replaced by another driving emotion: the need to understand. I needed to face her and ask her why. I needed to know how someone could be so evil. I had been robbed of the satisfaction of having my revenge but I could not just do nothing. Jane was no longer my wife and mother to our children. She was a monster I could confront without fear. All affection I once had for her had been destroyed. It had been replaced by the foulest of emotions.

A wild animal inside me was threatening to get out of control. In quieter more calm moments I appreciated the irony. A monster had been unleashed in Jane and I too had one trying to get out.

I scheduled a visit for two days later. I was obliged to arrange a formal visit because Jane was still being kept under close supervision in solitary confinement. This was necessitated by her constant arguments and fights with other inmates. They said it was for her own protection but in truth it was more probably to help keep the peace. Jane had acquired the unpleasant characteristic of causing trouble often leading to violence. It seemed that most of the violence visited upon her was the result of her behaviour towards others. In the social pecking order of the prison Jane was near the top and feared.

The day of my visit found me sitting in the visitors room struggling with my feelings. As I looked round the room I reflected on the drab and depressing surroundings. Was this to discourage visitors or perhaps set the tone for conversations? My thoughts were interrupted by the controlled chaos that ensued when the prisoners walked in, hunted around for their visitors and went to sat in the appropriate place.

Jane came in after all the other inmates escorted by a warder. She sat on the opposite side of the small table. I watched as patiently as I could fighting the anger inside. She looked unusually calm and alert but as usual said nothing. Though the noise around us was oppressive in the silence between Jane and myself I struggled to understand what to say. Small talk would have been an obscenity. I wanted to spend as little time as possible in her company. I needed to get straight to the point but how could I ask such an unspeakable question? But that is why I had come. I had to ask otherwise the torture of sitting in front of this evil woman would have been in vain. I had practised in my head what I would say and how I thought she would react. I was ready for it. I took a deep breath and looked her in eyes so bereft of warmth. She had a quizzical look on her face as if expecting my question.

"Why did you do it?"

Her eyes widened alarmingly as she blurted out a reply.

"Do what?"

"You know exactly what I mean. Why did you kill Angela?"

Jane's manner changed instantly. Her eyes bulged even wider and the muscles on her face tightened painfully. She looked like a deranged monster. Her usually quiet voice raged as loud as she could manage.

"What the hell are you talking about?"

I had expected this. I knew she would deny it much as she had been in denial over so much during the past year. But I was determined. She would own up to what she had done.

"I know it was you that persuaded Angela to commit suicide. Don't deny it, I have proof. You were hiding behind the alias Robert but I know it was you."

With a jolt Jane stood up came round the table and started to lash out at me in a frenzy. I put my arms up to defend myself as two wardens ran over and pulled her off. Grasping her arms tightly they led her away. In a last act of defiance she screamed back at me. She was still trying to make me the villain.

"Get that evil bastard away from me. He killed my daughter."

Another warden standing nearby signalled to me and I stood and left the room. As I walked along the corridor to the reception area my feelings were confused. I was satisfied I had confronted Jane but angry that she had neither acknowledged her crime nor given me any explanation. Not only had she denied it but had also tried to paint me as the wrongdoer. How could she do that? How could she come out on top of our confrontation?

Out in the reception area the woman warden that had befriended Jane was waiting for me. Smiling uncomfortably she waved me over to her.

"Hello Mister Cotter. Nice to meet you again. Can we have a chat?"

My immediate reaction was to tell her to go away. How could this stupid woman not see how evil Jane was? Curiosity caused me to relent and I followed her. How was she going to excuse Jane now?

We sat in a small room adjoining reception. Beyond the two chairs we sat on there was little else in the Spartan room. The prison authorities did not waste money on niceties. There was a look of deep concern on the warden's face.

"I have never seen Jane act like that. Do you know what caused it?"

I didn't care. I did not want to think about that evil person. I shrugged a little too emphatically causing a twinge of pain in my neck. In the stress I was enduring I had developed a lot of tension and the muscles were fatigued. A small movement caused them distress.

"You know how unstable she is. Perhaps seeing me reminded her of our loss. Maybe all her emotion came out at once."

"Possibly. Why did she accuse you of...sorry..that's a bit tactless."

"Why did she accuse me of killing Angela? Who knows what goes on inside her head? Perhaps she feels trapped and needed to lash out. I was there so fair game. Its your job to understand these evil people not mine."

I was sounding so convincing that I was starting to believe the lies I was spouting. A reality check shook me back to earth when I reminded myself it was Jane that had caused Angela's death.

The warden was nodding in agreement. She was believing the lies.

"She did say something very odd once. She talked about Angela going to a happier place. I presumed she meant Angela was going away or...well, I'm not sure what I thought really. In hindsight I wonder if...no, I'm sure I would have picked up on it. And surely she would have said something else..."

This internal debate she was having was annoying. Why didn't she say what she really meant? There was no point trying to spare my sensibilities. They had long since been blown away. The way to stop such insular thinking was to change it by asking a question. Dare I risk asking her about the Internet? I certainly did not dare to tell her what William and I had discovered. Equally I could not ignore it either.

"Are prisoners allowed to use the Internet?"

"On certain conditions yes. Why do you ask?"

"I have a suspicion Jane was talking to Angela?"

"What makes you suspect that?"

"Just a few things Angela said. As you know the children did not visit but Angela seemed to know things about Jane."

I was probing and playing a game. It was a lie but a lie no one could disapprove so I felt comfortable with it. If I could sow the seeds of some questions in this woman's mind perhaps they would investigate.

"We have placed even more restrictions on usage recently. There is some evidence that our systems are being hacked."

It was an almost casual comment but I was taken aback and my pulse quickened with shock. This was potentially disastrous news.

"Really? Any idea who?"

"The obvious answer is outside criminal activity. We suspect criminals were trying to stay in contact with each other. Probably working on the next crime when they get out. But I should not really be telling you this."

I did not care whether she told me or not. What I did care about was that I had to stop William doing anything more as soon as possible. I would need to do it in person. Paranoia told me that if the service were investigating, phone messages or emails could be tracked. These people knew what they were doing. They solved complex computer crimes.

My mind was still struggling to cope with the barrage. Every event assumed an exaggerated significance. This single thought erased all others in my mind and I needed to get away from the prison quickly. I made a great play of looking at my watch and feigning surprise.

"Goodness. Is that the time? You will excuse me but I must dash. I am late for a business appointment."

There was a look of surprise on the warden's face as I stood up quickly and thrust my hand in front of her. Confused she stood up, shook my hand and I walked away quickly cursing myself. Why had I behaved so impulsively? Surely I must have looked guilty? The paradox washed over me. It had come down to my looking and feeling guilty though totally innocent. I had behaved rationally my whole life but was now behaving differently. I left the prison in a state of panic and confusion. It was ridiculous. I was the victim in all this.

~ 28 ~

Months slipped by as I tried to rationalise the anger in my head. Slowly the realisation that I could do nothing made the rage seep away to be replaced by self pity. This was an emotion I despised when I saw it in others. Yet I was succumbing to it.

I sought comfort in the trivia of everyday life. I continued to excel at work with a resultant bolstering of our finances. It meant I could spoil Tom and indulge him in the long list of things he wanted. He had started proper school and was full of the new friends he made. In unguarded moments I could almost believe we were back to normality.

Winter came early, too early. I was not ready for the long dark nights. Nights always seem darker in Winter. Perhaps it is because they are longer. Does the brain get depressed with the long hours of darkness?

Does it start to switch off making everything seem so much duller? Then there is the cold. The body expends so much energy keeping warm that it depletes the reserves needed for the everyday things of life. Everything becomes so much more of an effort. What was it they called it, Seasonal Affective Disorder? The three letter acronym was singularly appropriate.

In past years we would have drawn closer as a family, spiritually and mentally cuddling against the cold. Somehow we would have managed to remain optimistic waiting for Spring. If I was down Jane would pep me up and I would do the same for her. And there was always the antics of Tom to amuse and cheer. He had immense ability to find mischief and bring a smile to us all. But this Winter would be different. Tom and I would have to face it on our own. We truly would be sad in all meanings of the word. I wondered whether it was worth investing in one of special lamps that were supposed to simulate sunlight to ward off SAD. Tom and I could sit and read by it in the evenings.

I decided to share the idea with Tom and let him decide. I needed to engage with him more often to keep his mind off the hell our life had become. If he liked the idea we would do it. I broached the subject over tea one evening.

"Should we go and buy a special lamp Tom?"

I had attracted his childish curiosity and he responded eagerly.

"Special how?"

"It pretends to be sunlight to cheer us up in Winter."

Tom was swinging his legs under his chair, a sure sign he was thinking.

"Is it magic then?"

"No, its scientific. It makes special light, that will make us feel better. Its a bit like sunshine indoors. You like the sunshine don't you?"

His legs began to swing more rapidly as he thought even harder.

"Could we take one for Mummy? She never seems happy. It might make her happy again. That would be good wouldn't it?"

I was full of admiration for Tom. Despite everything he still thought about his mother and cared. I had an absolute order in place permitting me not to take him to see Jane. He had not seen her for months but clearly still thought about her. He also still appeared to be hopeful that Jane would recover. Perhaps he hoped this magic lamp would help. Was it just the simple naivety of youth or something deeper? It would appear that he held no grudge for the way she had treated him. Or if he did he was hiding it well; certainly better than I was. Of course he was unaware of Jane's part in Angela's death. Perhaps I would tell him one day but for now it would not be of benefit to him.

It did concern me that he still cared for Jane and I searched my feelings trying to ensure that it was not jealousy. I did not feel comfortable yet trying to get him to face the truth. I needed to tread carefully. I needed to lie to him. His mind was far too young to cope with such evil. The shock would be too much. How could a five year old cope with such shattering news?

"We need to ask the men in the prison whether we can take a present in for her. They have lots of rules."

His face was a little disappointed but this passed quickly as he appreciated the logic in what I said. It was a welcome sign that he was growing up. He was now at the age where it was possible to reason and negotiate with him. He was still impetuous and illogical but was starting to change.

I knew this to be a deception. They would almost certainly not allow such a gift especially one with such a quirky association. Prison was no place for theories about sunlight causing depression. Life was much more basic inside. If a prisoner was depressed they simply gave them drugs. A comatose prisoner does not suffer depression. Above all prisoners were not allowed personal lights in their cells. And even if they were when the lights went out, they all had to go out.

I had dug a hole for myself and would need to think very carefully how to get out of it without upsetting Tom. I cursed the fact that life continued to play cruel tricks on me. I tried my best but somehow it kept kicking me. My judgement and choices seemed to be off track. My only sensible option was not to mention it again and hope Tom forgot about it.

It came as no surprise that life and Tom would not let me off that easily. A characteristic of children I had noticed with both Tom and Angela was that they had selective memories. If something interested them they would remember it and not let it go. If it did not interest them they would instantly forget it. Even when reminded it was if it never happened.

I was to find out over the next few days that regrettably Tom's selective memory had decided that the lamp was worth remembering. He pleaded constantly for us to go and buy the special lamps and eventually I had to give in. There are only so many times you can avoid answering a question and only so many excuses you can come up with for inaction. Tom was five and his youthful tenacity was now coupled with a stronger more capable mind. He no longer blindly accepted what I said but had started to form his own opinion. This made for some interesting battles between us. They were particularly challenging since I was still unsure of how hard I should be for fear of upsetting his fragile mind. I dare not risk pushing him away and making him introspective. I remembered how the stands I had taken with Angela had caused a gap between us. I was determined not to make the same mistake.

Even now Jane had a detrimental influence over us. Uncertainty followed me whenever we went shopping. The memory of Angela and the shop lifting incident still lingered in my memory. I kept Tom close by and watched his every move but he still had a habit of wandering off at speed. I am glad to say that he had stopped running everywhere but he still managed to move quickly once his mind was set on something. In an instant he would scurry off on a single minded mission. His normally wandering mind would adopt tunnel vision that drive a purpose.

As I examined the natural light simulation lamps I became aware that Tom was missing. He had run off elsewhere in the shop to look at something more interesting that had attracted his attention. Answering the panic that welled up in me I looked hastily around. On the opposite side of the shop I saw Tom talking with a young female shop assistant. She was laughing as Tom chatted excitedly to her.

I strolled over trying to look casual and allowing the panic to subside. As I approached the young woman looked up and eyed me with with great suspicion. In a high pitched voice and lazy tone typical of someone of her tender years she spoke coldly to me.

"Aren't you the husband of that awful woman who was in the news, the paedo? I saw you in the paper."

Memories of the awful fuss outside the courtroom came flooding back. The government campaign against child pornography was in full swing. All those awful photographers desperate to get a picture were unpleasant and aggressive. I feigned disdain but knew it was unconvincing. I really was a very poor liar.

"You are confusing me with someone else."

She scowled fiercely at me examining my face closely.

"No I'm not. You are him. The little boy told me his Mum was in prison. You just don't want to admit it. It was disgraceful what she did."

I looked at Tom but his mind was on other things. Mercifully this offensive rant appeared to be passing him by. I was desperately trying to protect him but life was still conspiring against us. Once again my hatred for Jane surfaced as I realised that this was something that would follow us for the rest of our lives. We would never be free. We could run, we could hide but it would always be there waiting to pounce on us. I would always be the husband of this evil woman and she would always be Tom's mother. Seeing us like this would make people comfortable. It would fit in with their view of the world.

Why did people take satisfaction from the misfortune of others? Was it some perverted desire to feel superior? Did they need to see everyone else as somehow worse than them to bolster their poor self esteem? When did sympathy for others die?

I grabbed Tom's arm and led him out of the shop. How was I going to explain this to him? Should I tell him the truth or try to protect him a little while longer? I loved his childish innocence and wanted it to continue for as long as possible. If only others felt the same way.

~ 29 ~

It was early evening and Tom and I had just finished tea. More accurately I had finished and Tom had picked at his. For some reason I could not fathom he had suddenly become a fussy eater. Until now he would eat anything put in front of him. He obviously had preferences for certain food but hunger always drove him to eat. Now he tended to pick at things he did not prefer but still seemed healthy and full of energy so I was not too concerned. I assumed he was going through one of those growing phases.

As I cleared the remnants of Tom's half eaten meal from his plate the door bell rang. These days it always made me jump. It was the same when the telephone rang; I always assumed the worse. No doubt it was a legacy from the early dawn raid and the shocking call from the police. Contact with the outside world seemed to bring only bad news.

Opening the door I saw the familiar face of Father Lucas who had visited last year. He smiled and spoke slightly awkwardly. His outstretched hand was left dangling. I wanted to know what he wanted before I extended a welcome. Father Lucas sensed my reluctance and slowly lowered his spurned hand.

"Nice to see you again Andrew. Sarah thought it would be a good idea if we met again, but if I am intruding then I will leave you in peace."

It was couched in that infuriating way that always irritated me. It was a reasonable request that would make me seem unreasonable to refuse. I recall that the priest had trained in psychology, was this a cheap trick he was playing? I cursed him silently. Rather than ringing or asking Sarah to ring he had turned up on my doorstep. It was an act of defiance. He had made the effort would I be so rude as to shun him? Did he talk so innocently to disarm me and make me feel obliged? Was it a form of blackmail? I realised that I was frowning and had not responded.

"Are you alright Andrew?"

I shook my head to clear my thoughts and managed to find a lie.

"Mm. Yes. I was just thinking about Tom."

"Tom? Nothing wrong I hope."

Despite the fact that I had bought Tom into our conversation I refused to be drawn into talking about him. Was he still trying to befriend me and gain my confidence? I would not play his game. I ignored the question and beckoned the priest inside.

"Come in. We have just finished tea so its not inconvenient."

Once again Father Lucas proffered his hand and I ignored it not out of malice but because my mind was pre-occupied. This was the man that had called Jane evil. He spoke things I did not want to hear. He had said she had a dark soul. In my perverse thinking somehow I associated his words with Jane's decline. It was almost as if I was blaming him. If he had not said anything then nothing would have happened. He had supported the blossoming of her evil.

Despite my own extreme feelings about Jane I could not countenance someone else telling me such things. I realised that he had the objectivity of the dispassionate man but I did not want to know. But at least he did not point with accusation or abuse me as the shop assistant had done the previous day. For that alone he deserved to be heard once more.

He looked ill at ease as he sat opposite me. Last time he had been calm and confident. As he started to speak I was concerned at what was on his mind. If such a self assured man was struggling I should be worried.

"When I was last here you were looking for answers. You wanted to know why this happened and whether Jane would get better. I confess I had no answers. We priests are often painted as all knowing with all the answers but its simply not true. What I believe we do have is understanding. Not total but at least partial. Have you heard to the Black Swan logical fallacy?"

"Vaguely. Its something to do with impossible events happening."

"More or less yes. Its more about events that could not be predicted. I believe that what happened to your wife is a Black Swan. It fits the criteria. It was a random event that could not be predicted and caused major disruption to your lives."

I was disappointed. Instead of constructive thoughts he was spouting some more of his home spun philosophy. I protested at what I saw was his attempt to put what happened into a box. Putting labels on things explains nothing. It is a trick to provide intellectual comfort to something we do not understand.

"That is just nonsense. Being bitten by a mosquito could have been predicted as could the possibility of picking up an infection. It happens in that part of the world. Similarly the affect on Jane's brain was a known problem with such an infection."

"But that is the point of Black Swan events. It is easy to rationalise them after the event. You could not have predicted that an apparently innocent holiday could lead to such a series of dramatic events."

"So how on earth does putting a label on it all help?"

"What happened was unpredictable. In the same way what will happen next is unpredictable. We cannot possibly predict what will happen to Jane next. Everything is being tried to cure her but it will be the unexpected that will make a difference."

This conversation was going nowhere and starting to annoy me. I had other things to do than waste time. Actually I did not have anything particular to do but still felt annoyed. I was familiar with the odd feeling that I could be doing something better without not knowing what.

"Where is this leading?"

"I think what I am saying is that Jane will only get better if something unexpected happens."

I was starting to get angry. He was conjuring up ridiculous solutions.

"How the hell does that help us?"

"It means that there is little point hoping that conventional methods will find a cure. It will need a Black Swan event. It will require something random and unpredictable."

"Such as?"

"That's the paradox. I have no idea. You cannot predict the unpredictable. All you can predict is its unpredictability. Sorry, that sounds trite doesn't it? Things often do when you put them into words."

I took a deep breath and released it slowly expressing my annoyance.

"This is a pointless conversation. You say you have an explanation which is just words and that you have an answer but have no idea what it is."

"Mmm, when you put it like that it does not sound very helpful. I am trying to find you some comfort..."

Now I really was getting angry. Who was this man to presume so much? Sarah had suggested he could help Jane not me. I did not want his comfort. I felt patronised.

"Did I ask you for some comfort? Save that for your flock. They might hang on your every word but I do not."

I wave of paranoia hit me. I instantly regretted my harsh words. What if he was working with social services? What if he was checking up on me to see if I was stable and capable of looking after Tom?

"Who sent you here? Are you working for someone?"

Anxiously the priest held up his hands.

"No. Well maybe...you know..."

He raised his eyes to the ceiling and smiled nervously.

"I was concerned that last time I came I was not much help. Actually I don't believe I was of any help at all. I just wanted to see if I could make amends."

He seemed genuinely concerned so my paranoia receded. Had I been too harsh? Perhaps I needed to redress the balance.

"Tell me, these Black Swan events, do you think they are divine intervention?"

"I'm not sure how to answer that. Its a bit of a loaded question. If I say yes then you could rightly ask: why does God intervene so maliciously?"

I shook my head and grunted.

"I know the answer to that. Its all part of the great plan."

"I presume you say that with some cynicism but I believe it to be true."

"I cannot accept that it was pre-ordained that my wife would get sick and turn into an evil monster. I cannot accept that it was pre-ordained that my innocent daughter would be so corrupted as to take her own life. How the hell does that make sense in any grand plan? What sort of perverted evil mind could concoct such a plan and to what purpose? And don't say to test me because that is crap. How can others suffer so that I can be tested? That is just malicious. I am no more special than the people who have been hurt."

An awkward silence fell between us which was broken by the softly spoken voice of the priest.

"I believe that Black Swan events happen in Gods plan. I believe that even he cannot predict these events. In a complex universe the random and unpredictable will happen."

"So what you are saying is that the grand plan is flawed."

"Possibly. I am not party to the whole plan. I only see the small fragment that represents my life and those around me. Its a very small window into a vast Universe."

"I don't mean to be rude but your smug view of the world is rather irritating and not at all helpful. What is the real point of your visit?"

Father Lucas sat breathing slowly and considering his reply. There was obviously something on his mind he was struggling with.

"I was wondering whether I could have your permission to visit Jane in prison?"

"Why? What purpose do you think it would serve?"

"I am not sure it would serve any purpose but I do believe that we must try as many things as we can. Maybe we can make a Black Swan event happen."

"But you said they are unpredictable."

"And they are but I also believe that you can create the circumstance in which they can happen."

"And you think you can create the circumstances?"

"Perhaps."

I felt deeply cynical. This man was starting to annoy me.

"With God's guidance?"

"Perhaps."

I shook my head disparagingly.

"You are making this up as you go along."

"That is life. None of us is aware of the plan for our lives. We all have to make it up."

"But you told me everything was pre-ordained...OK, I get it: everything apart from Black Swan events."

I shrugged my shoulders. I wanted this conversation to end.

"Do what you like. Why do you need my permission?"

"Sarah suggested I ask. Its a matter of courtesy. No its more than that, I wanted to know if you thought it would help. And I do not want to intrude where I am not welcome."

Damn him, he was being reasonable again. How could I reject such a reasonable approach? He was casting a die I could do nothing about without appearing unreasonable.

Just then Tom entered the room, frowned at the priest, turned and walked out again. The priest smiled at me.

"He's having a senior moment at his age."

"No its more likely he was dreaming up some mischief and your presence put him off."

Slowly the priest rose from his chair.

"That is probably my cue to go. I would not want to interfere with Tom's mischief."

He departed with an awkward air between us. I knew he meant well but he seemed clumsy. A very small part of me was curious to know how it would go with Jane but most of me did not care. If he wanted to try and save that evil woman, good luck to him. Perhaps it would give his life some purpose.

~ 30 ~

Jane had been placed in extreme isolation which meant no outside visitors were allowed. Once again there had been several tussles with other prisoners and it was decided Jane had started the fights. She was not even allowed contact with other prisoners in the isolation wing. Considering how she had effectively isolated herself in our house I would have thought she would have welcomed the solitude.

Despite the isolation she had once again turned violent and had to be restrained and sedated. Attacks on the warders were bad enough but use of drugs had been justified on the grounds of concerns over self harming. The authorities had noticed the tell-tale scars on her arms. Reality was that sedation made life much easier for the prison. How much it helped Jane was questionable. If the real Jane were still somewhere inside she would not be able to emerge through a drugged haze. In truth the drugs were killing any possibility of Jane recovering. They were driving her deeper into her psychosis.

During this period she was not allowed any visitors so neither myself nor the priest could attend. I had started to visit her occasionally again. It was a living hell to be in her presence but I had made a rod for my own back. By keeping quiet about my knowledge of Jane's part in Angela's suicide it was impossible for me to explain why I could not visit. I was still concerned about my image of a caring responsible person. I was desperate to ensure there was no question of my suitability to look after Tom. I was obliged to play the part of the dutiful husband offering comfort to a bereaved mother. I hated myself for this. I hated the system for driving me to this. I turned my anger onto anything I could.

With Jane's isolation came an uncomfortable sense of relief that I was temporarily spared the awkward visits. We would sit for about half an hour not speaking and avoiding eye contact. Each visit was made worse by the fact that often other prisoners would point at us and whisper to their visitor. Jane had attracted unwelcome notoriety.

I could see no point in such visits but had been assured by the prison authorities that it was an essential part of her rehabilitation. I was not convinced but felt I needed to show some support. I feared that if I detached myself too much the busy bodies still interfering in our lives would make something uncomfortable of it. Perhaps they would suspect me of becoming unstable too with ramifications for Tom.

In truth I had lost all feelings of affection for Jane and did not feel she deserved my support. She was responsible for the mess in which she found herself and worse, was responsible for the mess in my life. She was responsible for the death of our daughter. How could I offer support for someone so evil? I could not however fault the reasoning that if I were to abandon her then she would truly be lost. If there was a way back it could only be through people she trusted. We may never again have a life together but she was still a human being deserving of help. I cursed Father Lucas and his conscience. These things were so easy for him to say. Any rejection on my part made me a lesser person.

I took the opportunity of this welcome break to go away for a holiday with Tom. We had not had a holiday for a long time. It was something normal people in normal families did. We were most certainly neither but perhaps indulging in normal activities would help bring us back to something approaching normality. I was clutching at straws again.

Each day the thought of Jane ticked away in both our minds like some nasty virus attacking our thoughts. Tom did not harbour the same malicious thoughts but I could see the thought of Jane had started to sit uncomfortably with him. He was still expecting her to come home and her continued absence frustrated and annoyed him. His friends had mothers who stayed at home. Jane's continued absence singled him out as odd. His new school friends were starting to taunt him.

But there was another reason Tom was losing his affection for Jane. Slowly, almost imperceptibly I had started to turn Tom against her. It was impossible for me to decide whether this was right or wrong but felt compelled to do it for his own safety. A break meant we could fill our minds with new things to think about. It would be a change from the repetitive drudgery that was our day to day life. It would take us away from the constant tension of worrying that some other new disaster was lurking just round the corner.

I knew that taking Tom out of his school would cost me. Our lame government had introduced a system of fines for missing school. Their stupid belief was that children could not afford to miss any education. In truth they were ignoring the real problem. It was not the amount of time but the poor quality of the eduction children received. In practice Tom learnt more from me in the few hours we spent together in the evening than he learnt in several days at school. In more settled times I would have considered home education. Jane would have been more than capable of taking this on.

I had no reservations about taking him out of the failed school system. His education would not suffer one iota. At that moment in time I was more concerned about his character development than his education.

I considered several options both at home and abroad but settled for England. I wanted to show him more of his homeland. In the words of the vernacular I hoped it would give him some grounding in who he was and where he lived. There was a bigger and more interesting world out there than home and school. He had seen the inside of hospitals, police stations and prison. He needed to learn that these places had little significance in the wider world.

I decided I would try to show him some permanence in the uncertain world that was his life so far. We would drive down to the West Country exploring ancient monuments on the way such as Stonehenge and Glastonbury. He would learn that not all things are transient and unreliable, that some things are more permanent. In his short life things were changing so fast but there were things that did not change.

I took several days planning our route and investigating places to stay. As effectively a single parent the options were limited but it was out of the peak season so some places were happy to accommodate us. I was finalising the plan one early afternoon when the phone rang. I stared at it hoping it would stop. Why pick it up? It would only be bad news.

On the other end of the line was the social worker. I had not heard from her for some time and was beginning to hope she would not pester us again. Surely she must have had more pressing cases than ours? You read so many awful stories about disadvantaged families and bullying parents.

"We haven't spoken for a while so I thought I would give you a quick call to see if everything is OK."

Instinct told me there was more to it than a social call but I refrained from showing the anger I was feeling. I was still very wary of these people and their power to wreck lives.

"Yes, we are doing well, thank you."

"Good, good. I understand you want to take Tom out of school."

So that was the reason for the call. Someone had been telling tales. Why couldn't people mind their own business?

"Yes. I want to take him away for a few days just to give him a change of scenery."

"Has something happened? Is Tom alright?"

"Nothing has happened and Tom is fine. Everyone needs a holiday now and then."

"I have to say that I am not entirely happy with you taking time out of school. We must not let his education suffer."

"Are you saying I cannot do it?"

"No, just expressing some concern."

I could not longer exercise restraint. My pent up anger was starting to get the better of me.

"You're concerned that he will be spending some valuable time with his father? You are concerned that he will be seeing a different side of life? You are concerned he will be out in the fresh air enjoying himself. Frankly I am concerned that you are so concerned. I thought you had Tom's best interests at heart."

There was silence on the other end of the phone. It sounded like she had covered the mouthpiece blocking out even the hubbub of the office. I guessed she was talking to someone else, possibly her manager.

"You will need to let us know where you are in case we need to contact you."

"You have my mobile phone number."

"Yes but what if you do not have it switched on or lose it or the battery is flat? You could be in a poor reception area."

"Good grief. So what exactly do you need from me, a complete, detailed itinerary?"

My obvious sarcasm was lost on her as she responded almost mechanically.

"That would be perfect yes."

I took a deep breath and cursed quietly to myself. I had been absolved of any blame attached to what had happened and still they did not trust me. Jane was out of harms way and I strictly monitored Tom's activities on the computer. He did not use social networks or emails so was not exposed to the same dangers as Angela. The potential bullying issues Tom was experiencing at school were being sorted. What more did these wretched people want? I had to control myself. They were almost certainly still looking for any signs of instability in me. A temper would be one of the warning signs. Bad tempered people are violent aren't they?

"OK, I will send a copy to you today."

I wanted to be rid of this woman so I lied. Events had turned me into a dishonest man.

"You will have to excuse me there is someone at the door."

"Ah right. Thank you for your time. Let's talk again soon."

My unspoken thought was: not if I can avoid it, but I decided to err on the side of politeness.

"OK, goodbye then."

She had put up less of a fight than I thought. Was she just going through the motions? Perhaps she was under instructions to query what I was doing and would report back to the school. Who knows what these people got up to? I was not convinced that they knew themselves most of the time. It would seem that I was not allowed to make decisions about what was right for my son without their interference. Was this our future? Would we never get back to normality? Once again the sinking feeling fermented inside me.

~ 31 ~

As the day grew closer for our trip I waited to see what life was going to throw at us to spoil it. I was convinced some new chaos was winging its way towards us. One of Father Lucas's Black Swan events was surely lurking waiting to pounce.

We were struggling to live our lives day to day. Plans were for normal people with normal lives. Plans were for people whose future looked secure and stable. Our lives were about fire fighting and wrestling with uncertainty. Plans were not for the likes of us; they were far too certain.

To say that the call was unexpected would be wrong. I knew something would happen; it was just a matter of time. Jane attracted problems like a flower attracts bees. On the other end of the line was a nameless person from the prison administration office.

Apparently names were never used to protect the people working there.

"I'm afraid your wife has been involved in an incident. She has been admitted to hospital."

My reaction was odd. I felt detached, almost uninterested and accepted the news without question. After the long unpleasant sequence of events nothing surprised me. In fact it was almost as if I expected it. It was a logical event in a series of illogical events. Jane had been living by the sword and this was the consequence. A peculiar sense of justice entered my head. I found myself thinking that Jane deserved to be punished. It went some way to redressing the imbalance she had caused in our lives. I felt vaguely ashamed to think that way but could not prevent it. Not only was my life no longer mine to control, neither were my thoughts and feelings. Emotions drove my thinking and those emotions were no longer under my control.

Despite these odd feelings I still retained some vestige of affection for her. It was hidden and very faint but would not go away. Perhaps it was just a habit I could not break. We had once shared a loving relationship. We had had two children. If I thought hard and dug deep enough into my tainted memory I could recall many good times we had shared. I owed her some loyalty. She was not to blame for her condition. It was not her fault. And in moments of honesty and self pity the nagging doubt that I was to blame would not go away.

Father Lucas talked about pre-ordained destiny and fate, but he was wrong. Our lives are driven by the decisions we make. Everything would have been so different if we had gone to the South of Spain as Jane would have preferred. One small insect seeking food had ruined our lives. Its search for sustenance to produce its own young had wrecked the lives of others. It was an innocent act. It had no idea that its natural act would have such awful consequences.

In strictly matter of fact tones the nameless administrator explained that Jane had been set upon by other prisoners. She further explained that they have a perverse sense of right and wrong. Stealing, mugging, burglary, shop lifting, these are all acceptable as part of their lives. But they believe child pornography to be wrong. It is a most peculiar set of standards but who can understand the criminal mind? Their sense of right and wrong is skewed and alien to the likes of me. I knew all this but listened patiently while she read the script.

Jane had been taken to the local hospital. Though she was under protective guard I was given permission to visit her. She was after all the victim this time and deserving of the sympathy and support due to any victim. What could not be denied was that fact that if she had not committed her crimes in the first place then she would not have been in prison and therefore in danger. Surely even Father Lucas could not deny that her fate was determined by her own actions? She was a blip in the grand plan.

Later that day I left work early to visit the hospital. Walking through the main entrance a strange sense of foreboding stifled me. As I entered Jane's room memories of the hospital in Kenya came flooding back. Again a sense of guilt came over me. This was all my fault.

I stood looking at the unconscious woman. Though older and care worn in calm sleep she looked much more like the woman I married. Had I just woken from a nightmare? The presence of a prison guard sitting nearby reminded me of the reality. As I entered she rose to meet me.

"Mister Cotter?"

"Yes."

"I will fetch the doctor to come and talk to you."

As she walked across the room I continued to stare at the motionless woman.

"Wasn't she in isolation?"

"Yes, but it is impossible to keep someone isolated one hundred percent of the time. They have to shower, use the toilet etc. A prison cannot be run for the sake of one person."

"Surely every individual is important?"

In a cold matter of fact way she shook his head. Her face adopted a cold dispassionate appearance. She had clearly suffered in her job and that had made her hard.

"No one asks anyone to go to prison. It's their choice. They commit the crime. They must take the consequences."

It was clear from the way she spoke that he had no time for Jane. The tone in her voice showed contempt. I was angry but managed to control myself.

"You almost seem to be endorsing what happened."

She shook his head again with more emphasis. Perhaps she realised he had spoken out of turn.

"Of course I'm not. I'm just saying its an unfortunate consequence. I'll be back in a minute."

The doctor was brief and cold in his explanation. Did I detect some contempt in him as well? Perhaps he had dealt with too many similar incidents involving prisoners and his tolerance had been eroded. He had more deserving cases needing his attention.

They were still carrying out tests to establish exactly what damage the beating had done. It had apparently taken the guards several minutes to be alerted to what was happening and in that time the other prisons had been very severe in their punishment. Their own incarceration built up much anger and frustration they readily took out on Jane.

In what I appreciated was a thoughtful act of consideration the guard left me alone with Jane and waited outside. In truth she was probably glad to be away from this woman she despised. This assignment was a pleasant change from the stress of her normal duties. It was now made even more enjoyable by strolling free from responsibility.

After several hours sitting and watching the peaceful woman I fell asleep. I awoke to see a dark shadowy figure hovering near her bed beckoning me. It was the shadow from my recurrent dream; the shadow that was trying to steal my children. He had stolen one, was he now after the other? Or was he after me? I violently shook my head to clear the image and the figure faded into the distance. It had only been my imagination but none-the-less frightening.

With the acceptance that I needed to abandon the trip with Tom, my hatred and loathing grew again. The faint hint of affection faded. Even at a distance Jane was still ruling our lives.

I had been granted permission to take Tom to see his mother. It had been a scrap with the social worker. It was felt that a prisoner in hospital was not a fitting place to take a young impressionable boy, especially as Jane's face was a mess. And then there was the effect of Jane's behaviour. The conditions laid down by the court were very clear. Tom was to live with me but have no contact with his mother. But following assurances from the doctor that Jane was in a deep coma and absolutely no danger she had conceded. I argued that since Jane was not awake there was no real contact. It was a tenuous argument but I won through eventually.

I was instructed not to let Tom out of my sight and certainly not to leave him alone with Jane. Much as my rebellious instincts reacted against these dictatorial instructions I complied without giving voice to my objections. I had learnt that fighting these people was counterproductive. They wielded absolute power and delighted in it. If you were not with them you were a problem and they had harsh ways of dealing with problems. Whatever my violent private thoughts and objections absolute compliance was the only way to communicate with them. Do otherwise and they could make life very difficult.

As Tom and I sat in silence watching Jane the doctor entered the room. Pausing he nodded at Tom.

"Is it alright to speak in front of your son?"

I stood up and looked at Tom who seemed to be in one of his many dream worlds. I wondered which one it was, superhero, lorry driver, spaceman, rampaging monster? I moved closer to the doctor so that he could speak more softly.

"Of course. What have all your tests found out?"

A peculiar expression was fixed on the doctor's face. His normal confident self assurance seemed to have vanished. He was puzzled.

"There is nothing clinically wrong. She just seems to have switched off."

"Switched off?"

"Yes. I am sorry to be so vague but its very strange."

Tom had come over to my side and was grasping my hand tightly.

"Is weird Mummy sleeping?"

I looked at the Doctor slightly embarrassed and then down at Tom's innocent concerned face.

"Yes. She is tired."

He seemed satisfied with the explanation but in an instant his face twisted into a look of anguish.

"When she wakes up will the old Mummy come back or will she still be weird Mummy?"

In a simple question he had encapsulated all our fears and a dark part of my soul hoped she would not wake. Even if the old Jane came back would I have any feelings for her beyond hate and loathing? I had seen into Jane's dark soul which it seems had always been there and would always be there. Even if the Jane Tom and I knew came back we now lived in a different more threatening world. There would be this dark stranger lurking in the background waiting for the chance to emerge, waiting to take away the remnants of my life.

At that moment I felt Tom and I to be in the greatest of dangers.

~ 32 ~

Whilst ever Jane remained in the coma she was to stay in hospital under guard. I struggled to resolve the conflict in my mind as to whether it was right for Tom to visit. I took him that first time but did not want to take him again. I did not want to take any risks. He saw that Jane was not well and that seemed to satisfy him. It explained her absence.

But I was coming under pressure. Everyone told us how important the relationship between a mother and child was but seemed to overlook the particular circumstances. Surely they could see that Jane had the potential to cause harm? I had already fought this battle. Why was it being brought up again?

I had the security of a court order to hide behind but conceded to the pressure. Tom's reaction when I told him we were going to see Jane in hospital again was strange. He wavered between the excitement of the adventure and the fear he had developed for Jane. After much thought he blurted out a question.

"Will he be there?"

"Who?"

"The dark man."

How could I answer with any honesty? I knew that Tom was still seeing the apparition or whatever the hell he was. He did not talk about it. Perhaps he no longer feared him. He certainly seemed able to talk about him so I tried not to show my concern.

"I don't think so. But if he is we will tell him to go away."

"OK. I don't like him. He's horrible."

This seemed to satisfy him though my own mind was in turmoil. This was not the first time I had made this assurance. I kept promising to make this thing go away but in reality I could not. Surely Tom would stop believing my false promises? He was in an uncertain world that had all but collapsed about him. I was his last and only resort for answers to impossible questions. It was a difficult burden to carry. Honesty was not always the right option. However careful I was it was certain I would get it wrong eventually.

It was late afternoon when I had picked Tom up from school and we drove to the hospital. Jane was still in the isolation room and apparently still in a coma. A strange contradiction filled my head. I was glad she was still not awake since we would not have to talk to her. But I also wanted her to be awake so I could take Tom away. That was the deal. I was absolutely adamant there would be no communication.

Seeing her lying motionless did not appear to be upsetting Tom but he was certainly not quite his normal excitable self. He stayed completely silent during our visit and it was some considerable time afterwards that the excitable character reappeared seeking out new mischief to amuse himself.

I convinced myself his silence was an effect of the hospital itself rather than Jane's situation. I had learnt a great deal of self delusion over the last six months. The more I was creative with the truth to Tom the more I felt at ease deluding myself. It was not so much a means of keeping sane as of avoiding facing reality. If it was the hospital upsetting him rather than Jane it was more easy to accept.

I reaffirmed my resolve that once Jane was awake I would no longer take him. I did not want her anywhere near him. This thought troubled me. What was I to do once Jane was released from prison? Could I stop her getting anywhere near Tom? Surely the courts would grant an exclusion order against her?

Deeply troubled I contacted my solicitor and he promised to investigate the options I had. For my part I only saw one option, complete exclusion, but he believed I would probably have to compromise and allow limited but supervised access. Courts steadfastly supported the rights of mothers even under extreme circumstances. The wishes of the father were almost irrelevant. Mothers were given second chances not granted to fathers.

I vowed to fight this tooth and nail and with whatever else I could. As far as I was concerned Jane was lost to us for good. There was too much to forgive. I did not want her to return. I wanted Tom to forget about her and I certainly did not want to be anywhere near her. If I was pushed to the limit I would expose what I had found out about her involvement in Angela's suicide. There would be risks with awkward questions to answer but Tom's safety was paramount.

Tom and I were settling down for the night. He had been unhappy about something all day but steadfastly refused to explain. I suspected it was something to do with school since he was showing increasing reluctance to go. Was he still being bullied? The school had promised to look into it. Perhaps they had not bothered. I knew how difficult it was for a school to suggest to a parent that their precious child was a bully. There had even been cases of parents attacking teachers as a result.

I determined to pay a visit and investigate. Normally I simply dropped him off and went. Tomorrow I would go inside with him and talk with his teacher. If the other children were giving him a hard time I would insist once more on remedial action. He had been through enough already in his short life. There was already too much I could not control, school would not become another factor. They would have to stand up to the bullying and the parents.

Though Tom continued to be reluctant to go to bed I insisted. I sat on the end of his bed whilst we chatted about lots of things, mostly trivial but assuming significance in our mutually stressed minds. Several times his eyes shut and he opened them again with a start fighting the inevitable oncoming sleep. I gently stroked his forehead and spoke in soft tones. Finally exhausted he fell asleep.

It was gone midnight when the phone rang. I was starting to despise the device absolutely. It only ever bought bad news. Tonight was to be no different. It was the police again. Would there be no end to their interference?

"Mister Cotter, its Sergeant Vinall from the police. I am sorry to trouble you at this time but I have to tell you that your wife has escaped from custody."

After all that I had been through bad news no longer had the same effect on me. It was beginning to be a normal part of my life. What should have shocked me had little impact. I was developing a detachment from the real world which should have worried me. This was how Jane behaved. Of course she had escaped. It was a logical consequence. Surely the authorities must have been expecting it?

"How was this possible. Wasn't she guarded?"

"The doctors assured us she would be in the coma for the foreseeable future so the prison guard was taking a break. They are short of resources and do not have the people to guard one prisoner round the clock."

"But wasn't the room locked? Wasn't she locked to the bed?"

"Yes, but somehow she managed to unpick the locks and get free."

Questions raced around my head and I shouted them down the phone.

"Didn't anyone notice? Wasn't she on monitors? Wouldn't one of the nurses notice that the monitors had stopped working?"

A calm voice replied. Perhaps he was accustomed to dealing with excitable people. He was delivering a message not offering himself for interrogation.

"Its very strange. They tell us the monitors were still working even when your wife was no longer attached to them. It was some sort of fault in the equipment."

Still the questions raged. It was starting to sound implausible.

"What about CCTV, was there any sign of her?"

"Yes. It looks like she had some help but we cannot make out who it was. The pictures are very dark."

I gasped as the implications sank in. Did she have help from the dark stranger? I shook away the ridiculous thought. He was just a figment of my imagination.

"So what happens now?"

"Obviously there is a search. We doubt she will get far. Her injuries have not completely healed. If she tries to contact you, you must let us know immediately."

"Of course. Do you think she will come here?"

"I don't believe she has anywhere else to go unless you know of somewhere?"

"There's her sister but they don't really get on now. Do you think we need some protection?"

Vinall paused, I could almost hear him thinking.

"Everyone I have available is out looking. We will be keeping an eye on your house. A patrol car will pass regularly. I will get someone to call round in the morning. Meantime I'm sure there is nothing to worry about. I will call you tomorrow."

Abruptly the phone went dead. Maybe he wanted to avoid any more awkward questions. His last comment screamed insincerity. It was an obvious and unconvincing lie. Of course there was something to worry about. I sat for several minutes trying to let my mind assimilate everything. Would this ever end with Jane? I went upstairs and looked in on Tom. He was still sound asleep. He looked so peaceful oblivious to the chaos that was going on around us. I envied him. In sleep he could escape everything that Jane, the school and life in general could throw at him. My own sleep was not so peaceful.

I double checked the front and back doors. It was unnecessary since I had become obsessive about our safety. Locking the doors tight each night symbolised shutting out the cruel outside world. I usually carried this out with Tom as a way of giving him a sense of security. We were locking out all the nasty people. He counted each lock and at the end we agreed that all ten had been closed.

I studied some papers I had bought home from work until gone two o'clock. My mind finally settled down and stopped racing with wild thoughts and I felt ready for sleep. With one last obsessive check of the locks and Tom I retired to bed. Somehow that night we seemed less secure. Jane was wandering loose. She was capable of anything. Had she not shown that locks were no obstacle to her?

~ 33 ~

Tom was still sleeping in my room. I knew that at some point I would need to coax him into going back into his own room but the time never seemed quite right. My reluctance also owed something to the pleasure I got in not sleeping on my own. Was I avoiding the time for his sake or mine? Were we offering each other mutual comfort?

I would settle Tom in bed at about seven o'clock. Often it was a battle as he continued to fear the night time. It was also clear that the events of a the day troubled him and his mind was unsettled. There was definitely something wrong at school. But I had to get him into a routine and as close to a state of normality as possible. It was essential for his development. He could not continue falling asleep on me in front of the television, obliging me to carry him upstairs.

I had to call a halt. It was also important for me; I too needed some stability. Though I always won the battle of wills it gave me no satisfaction to see his distress. I would sit on his bed and chat until he drifted off to sleep again. I then needed to exercise the greatest care rising so as not to wake him. It was a ritual but I felt was essential for now.

I would go to bed some time after midnight dependent on the various things I needed to do around the house. Fortunately once Tom had gone to sleep in his bed very little disturbed him for the first few hours so I was able to potter around without worrying about the noise. There always seemed to be so much to do and a never ending list of chores. Though there was only two of us we somehow managed to create enough mess for many more. I tried to instil a culture of tidying up as we went along but in truth I was as bad as Tom. Without my regular evening clear up the house would have been a disgrace. Tidiness and order were an important part of Tom's normality and indeed mine. There was also some comfort in the regimentation of restoring order. It was a substitute. If only I could have done the same to our shattered lives.

My own sleep pattern was very disturbed. It would take me some time to fall asleep as my brain buzzed with thoughts. Each night the same thoughts and questions would torture me as I failed to find any solutions to the mess that was our life. Once asleep I would wake several times and look over to the peacefully sleeping boy. He was providing some stability to my life though he himself was becoming increasingly disturbed. He was still energetic and excitable but this would be punctuated with an increasing number of periods of silence. Of course I expected him to calm down a little as he grew up but it was more than this. Something else was affecting his behaviour.

In the restless hours before sleep I often reflected on the fact that we had no friends. What friends I had were now avoiding me. I did not blame them for it must have been difficult to relate to what had happened. I could live with that since it also meant I did not need to put on the pretence that everything was fine. Friendship cannot exist in a lie.

I was more concerned at Tom's lack of friends. A lively five year old should have other children around him. It was important for his development especially developing how to interact with people. I was always the man in charge and not really a friend. I also could not get excited about his battered toy rabbit in the way another child of his age could. Would this stunt his emotional development? Many times I cursed Jane for her continued damaging affect on our lives. I could not move on since she was still present. And there was the ever present future threat of her release.

Two days after the news of Jane's escape Tom was being particularly difficult. Having made progress in persuading him to go to bed more easily this evening he had reverted back to being difficult. He seemed to be scared about something but would not say what. My daily cleaning had been punctuated by a number of dashes upstairs to answer distressed calls from Tom. I comforted him then went back downstairs to carry on my duties. This happened five times before at last he fell into a deeper sleep. It was two o'clock in the morning before he had finally gone to sleep and I had crawled exhausted into my own bed.

Exhaustion saw me fall asleep quickly without the usual rambling in my brain. However it was not long before I was having a typically disturbed dream, this time about a giant rabbit typing on a computer. It was chatting on social media to some mosquitoes, plotting who to bite. As absurd as it sounded in daylight, it seemed harshly realistic whilst asleep. I was awoken by Tom shaking my arm urgently.

"Daddy, there's someone outside."

I woke and turned to look at the face of the frightened boy. His eyes were wide open and he was looking toward the half open door.

"Outside where?"

"On the landing outside the bedroom."

I listened carefully but could hear nothing. Was Tom dreaming or were his ears more sharp than mine? I sprang out of the bed, walked towards the door and out onto the landing. To my shock at the far end I saw Jane shuffling towards me. She walked as if her body were too heavy for her legs. Her breathing was loud and laboured. As I stared at the awful sight I noticed she was not alone. Standing behind her was the dark stranger almost as if her shadow. It seemed to be holding her up and pushing her forward. In a voice that was not Jane's I heard her scream.

"We have come for the boy."

Tom was standing behind me holding onto my leg. I grabbed the sobbing boy who was shaking violently with fear. With a force I had never used on him before I dragged him away and into the back room that had once been Angela's bedroom. Slamming the door shut I knelt down to comfort Tom.

"I will not let them get you."

Tom grabbed me firmly round the neck and wept profusely. Unable to speak he sobbed making strange almost inhuman noises. My anger reached furious proportions. This was the final straw. I was not going to tolerate any more from this evil woman. She was not my wife, she was something sub-human.

I stood and looked down at the sobbing boy filled with compassion and rage.

“Tom when I go out put this chair against the door. Don't let anyone in unless its me. Do you understand?”

“Please don't go Daddy.”

His heartfelt plea cut straight to my heart but I knew what had to be done. We could not continue our lives under this threat. It had to end once and for all.

“I must make these evil people go away. I will be back as quickly as possible.”

I re-entered the hallway to see Jane standing like a statue and fixing me with a wild stare. Behind me I could hear Tom wrestling with the chair trying to block the still partially open door. Again the stranger's voice yelled at me.

“You will not stand in our way.”

I had assured Tom I would make them go away but had no idea what to do. This was something from a nightmare that had no obvious resolution.

“Whoever you are you will not win. I will not let you. Go away now or I will make you.”

Jane flew at me like a wild animal. I stepped aside and pushed her away. Stumbling she tripped and fell sprawling down the stairs. With a sickening crunch she landed at the bottom. I stood on the landing staring down at her lifeless body. As my eyes grew accustomed to the half light I saw the dark figure squatting next to her lifeless body. I recognised the figure as the man that had haunted us for so long. Raising his head the figure glared wildly at me with a look of pure hatred. It was the first time I had seen his face and the look of hate and evil would stay with me forever.

Uncertain as to what to do I sat down and breathed slowly trying to regain some sense of reality. I should have gone down to see if Jane was alright but I did not care. As I stared at the scene below the realisation swept over me: I did not care. I sat for several minutes in a trance trying to shut out the horror I had just been through. My meditation was disturbed by the soft plaintive cry of Tom.

"Daddy. Are you still there?"

Shaken instantly back to reality I rose and went to the room I had left Tom. I gently tapped on the door.

"Tom. It's alright. You can let me in."

I heard the scrapping of the chair as he wrestled to move it and the door slowly opened. Mercifully he could not see to the bottom of the stairs and I ushered him to stay in the room. As we both sat in the bed I picked up the phone and dialled. Seconds later a voice answered and I coldly replied. It was not me that spoke. I was simply an actor in a terrible tragedy.

"I need the police and an ambulance."

~ 34 ~

After a short hearing the coroner returned a verdict on Jane of accidental death. The judgement came as a relief since it meant an end to the suspicion and interrogation to which we had been subjected.

For nearly two weeks the police had questioned both Tom and myself on and off about the incident. It was obvious they were suspicious and they made no pretence of trying to hide their thoughts. But Tom's constant repeating that Jane tripped and fell finally convinced them I was innocent of anything untoward. Meanwhile our social worker had insisted that the police stop talking with Tom and even went so far as obtaining a court order to prevent them bullying him any further. It was the first act by this woman I deeply resented I had applauded. I had misjudged her. She really did seem to have Tom's interests at heart.

Equally as important it would seem that she did trust me.

Tom made no mention of my pushing Jane away. I could not recall whether he had managed to close the door but I presumed that in the confines of Angela's bedroom he had not seen what actually happened. I wanted to believe this was the case otherwise the alternative was too terrible to contemplate. He would have to live with the knowledge of having seen his father push his mother to her death however unintentionally. He was probably still too young to completely grasp the difference between an intentional act and and an unintentional consequence. But one day his mind would be able to make sense of it.

If I was being brutally honest with myself I never understood whether my action was intentional. I knew I felt a great sense of relief that something had come to an end but precisely what that something was I could not grasp. Jane would still be influencing us for the rest of our lives. Perhaps I was symbolically trying to push this influence away.

Of course that influence would have diminished with time but the damage would remain with us. She had set a course for the rest of our lives and we could do nothing to change that. She had given us a sight of evil which would taint everything else in our lives. We would live with the threat that evil could suddenly come from anywhere, even the most innocent of people. Evil was not necessarily something distant; it could be very close. As he grew older would Tom harbour the suspicion that I too could suddenly turn and become evil? It had happened to his mother, why not his father? Perhaps he would never trust anyone again.

I felt a great sadness for Tom that with this final episode the evil was probably all he would remember of his mother. In later years would he have been too young to remember the real Jane or was the memory lurking inside? Would he be able to recall the loving and affectionate mother? I wanted somehow to show him what Jane had really been like but had been warned that the Jane he knew would by too strong in his memory. The most recent memories are always the most potent especially in young children, Perhaps when he was an adult he would be able to cope with the memories. I hoped that by then he would have all but forgotten about what happened but accepted that it would almost certainly meaning forgetting about Jane.

Then there was Angela, how much would he remember about her? I never told him about what happened. All he knew is that Angela had gone away but it was clear that he missed her. At first he would ask when she was coming back. But in time the questions would fade as he accepted his lonely fate. It was inevitable that Angela and Jane would become distant memories as the more immediate things of growing up filled his mind. How many of us remember things that happened when we were four or five? They become buried deep in our memory though can still have an effect on us as we grow. We are all moulded by things we have forgotten.

It was two years later when Tom was seven I became concerned that he was still introspective and subject to waking in the night with bad dreams. We had finally been freed from the social worker. In their magnanimity they had decided I was a fit parent and that Tom was safe in my care. We were also no longer receiving support from the police family liaison organisation. We had finally been left to get on with our lives in what for us passed as peace. The shocking events of our lives had passed into history and no longer of concern to anyone but us. The case files were confined to the archives probably never to see the light of day again.

I was overwhelmed by a sense isolation. Indeed in truth Tom and I were alone. I had lost touch with anyone in either my or Jane's family and my friends seemed to have vanished. Sarah's promise to stay in touch had proved empty and I was reluctant to pursue her. She was a reminder of what had happened. What would we talk about? I certainly was not prepared to bare my soul to someone I hardly knew.

With Jane and Angela gone our lives had lost a large part of their meaning. Of course I missed Angela desperately and in unguarded moments I even missed Jane. Whilst she had still been alive there was always the lingering hope she would come back to us. Now even that futile hope was gone. Much as I loved Tom he could not fill the void completely, and I knew that for my part I could not fill the hole in his life. I was not his mother or sister and I could not erase the memory of what had happened from his mind. I would come to terms with it, but would he? We would both be haunted for the rest of our lives.

At work I had switched into mechanical mode. Nothing seemed important and I did what was necessary. I became increasingly intolerant of the politics and back stabbing frequently exploding in bad temper and ranting at colleagues. Aware of my situation my bosses were patient but I knew it was only a matter of time before something had to give. They could not tolerate a disruptive influence in the confines of a busy office. They knew there were questions about colleagues behaviour but its was expected that we tolerate it. Every day the tension was in danger of erupting and I was adding fuel to the fire. To make matters worse I was no longer delivering the business. I had pillaged my territory and picked it clean.

I was assigned a different role but this only served to isolate and anger me even more. Being singled out for special treatment was both embarrassing and annoying. I had done nothing wrong. What was I being treated that way?

Tom was struggling at school. His increasing introspection meant that he paid little attention during lessons, a source of concern to his teacher. When we met to discuss her concerns I became very angry at her implied hints that perhaps he needed special help. She was suggesting that he was showing signs of being backward. I ranted angrily at her that what he needed was normality not special attention. She should get on and do her job properly. I expected more from someone I entrusted my child to.

I later regretted my outburst. We had got rid of the interfering social worker. The last thing we needed was for the school to report my behaviour and express concerns. I recall the social worker suggesting that quietness in children was often a sign that they were being bullied. Would they suspect his bad tempered father of being a bully?. I rang the school the following day to apologise and the teacher showed welcome understanding. Another crisis in our continuing saga of never ending crises had been averted.

I realised I was struggling to cope and decided to contact Father Lucas. Though I disagreed with much of what he said his calm understanding and eloquence might be of value to us. I felt deeply lonely. As a minimum he was someone I could talk to. I would not be obliged to be sociable or even polite. He would listen because it was his job. It was cynical but I had every reason to feel such a base emotion.

~ 35 ~

Father Lucas became a frequent visitor to our house. At first he would arrive under a pretext but as these became increasingly implausible he dropped them. There were only so many times he could just happen to be passing or bringing us some literature to read or collecting for a charity or whatever excuse he could come up with.

I finally called a halt to any more pretexts by inviting him to call whenever he wanted. Tom had warmed to the affable man and as long as Tom was happy I was content for him to visit. I was still ferociously protective of Tom and the priest presented no danger. In fact he seemed to be helping restore Tom back to his old boisterous self. He seemed to have his own mischievous child inside eager to come out as they engaged in games of rough and tumble. It was sometimes difficult to spot who was the bigger child.

It was an odd sight to see a man of the cloth wrestling with a small boy and readily accepting being punched and kicked. I had always chastised Tom when he punched or kicked when we played so I viewed the tussles with Father Lucas uncomfortably. Sarah had said he training in psychology so I was trusting that he understood how far to let Tom go without the risk of turning him into a bully. He later confessed to me it was a deliberate ploy to get Tom to trust physical contact with another person. Father Lucas was very perceptive. Though Tom and I frequently touched for many practical reasons he shied away from contact with other people.

Father Lucas would visit us two or three times a week in the early evening a couple of hours before Tom's bedtime. Once Tom had gone upstairs we would talk for about an hour before he left. We did not exactly become friends. He tended to maintain a professional distance showing suitable respect. He preferred to enact rough and tumbles in the mind with me.

Though it was clear to me he was curious to know more about us he never asked intrusive questions. Instead he possessed an innate ability to get me talking without asking questions. An almost casual comment would spark a reaction and a conversation would take on a life of its own. An odd remark or observation would keep the momentum going. To say he played devil's advocate seems inappropriate for a priest but is a close description of his style.

I had always fancied myself as a bit of a philosopher so it was fascinating to talk with this man who was himself a deep thinker. I had never trusted religion or religious thinkers. There was too much myth and deception. I could never accept unquestioning belief. I was not an atheist but in the words of the priest: a deeply cynical sceptic. I could not reconcile everything that had happened to us with a benevolent being. I most certainly did not accept that I was being tested. Why should such a test be at the expense of the lives of two people I loved? That was vicious and cruel in the extreme. This benevolent being must have a wicked streak to concoct such a plot. Unless it was the work of the devil in which case why had he chosen my family? But I had always believed that the devil was a figment of our imagination arising from fear of the unknown. It was a ruse to explain the inexplicable and uncomfortable.

Gradually the priest started to convince me that the devil did in fact exist. It was the only logical explanation for so much evil in the world. He believed that the devil acted as a counterbalance to God. It helped us keep a perspective on right and wrong. If we did not understand evil how could we appreciate what was good in life? It seemed too simple and cosy an explanation to me but was difficult to argue against especially with a man of such deep and unshakeable conviction. Contradicting him almost seemed like an offence against his person.

Jane's death freed Father Lucas of his obligation to observe confidentiality and he gradually told me of the conversation he had with Jane that had concerned him so much. We often spoke about good and evil. In fact it was present every time we spoke. We had seen much of both. Though most of his experience was through the eyes of others he had a profound understanding. One question kept circling in my mind and one night when we had both had a little too much wine I felt compelled to ask.

"I know I have asked this before but do you think she was possessed? This dark figure always seemed to be near her."

Looking up from his glass the priest looked at me with a seriousness I had seen once before. It was the time he told me Jane had a dark soul. I had cast a shadow over us and wanted to retract the question but it was too late. He took a deep breath and answered thoughtfully.

"No. I believe that what you were seeing was the projection of Jane's evil self."

It was a puzzling reply that needed further explanation. Surely he was not talking about astral projection? The church did not hold with such things.

"You mean it was my imagination?"

"Yes. Our minds are incredibly powerful. There are vast areas of it that are a mystery. We haven't even started to understand what it is capable of. We are constantly inundated with a myriad of information and somehow our brain must cope with it and make sense of it. There are many ways it can do this. Perhaps seeing things is one of them. Perhaps your mind interpreted what it saw as an evil possession."

"But projecting the image of someone who is not really there, is that possible?"

Pursing his lips he nodded in agreement. He had recently told me he believed that anything and everything was possible but there were natural checks and balances to control what happened. Sometimes these controls failed and when they did the unimaginable could happen.

"You say Tom also saw this figure?"

"Yes. In fact he saw it more than me."

"I believe we are all are born with heightened abilities that we grow out of. It is this ability that enables us to learn so much so quickly as babies. In fact it is essential that we have this ability. Its a question of survival. Think of young children. They can be seriously frightened of things they imagine. Adults often exploit and manipulate this as a way of controlling behaviour. If you don't behave the bogey man will come for you. It can strike terror into the minds of small children whose imaginations are so acute. But quickly the harsh realities of life force us to focus on coping and surviving. The creative parts of our minds are put to sleep. They are not necessary in our day to day lives. In fact they would get in the way. We cannot live in a dream world; that's far too risky. Lack of use of these abilities destroys them. However, something can happen to adults to reawaken these corners of the mind."

"Do you think that is what happened to me?"

"It is possible yes. Have you never day dreamed and seen things as if they were real?"

"Yes, but they are not real."

"But they seemed real at the time. To all intents and purposes they were real. The brain cannot always distinguish between reality and fantasy. In the absence of something tangible to latch on to there is no difference. The brain needs checks and balances to make sense of the world. Second by second our senses are bombarded by information. We cannot possibly cope with it all so we filter and screen it, even throwing some of it away. This process needs to work efficiently otherwise we would go mad."

"Aren't you talking about hysteria?"

"No. You do not seem to be a hysterical person. You appear to be very level headed. We are in a realm of the mind no one understands."

An eerie silence fell between us. I looked at the normally calm face of the priest. It had taken on a tortured appearance. Something was disturbing him. With a deep sigh he spoke quietly.

"I am not sure I should say this but Jane will always be in your mind. You must take care that she does not reappear."

"Do you mean that the dark figure may come back?"

I had thought the nightmare was over. But the simple nod of his head sent a chill down my spine.

~ 36 ~

In the ten years that have passed, our lives have attained something approximating to normality. At least, we have come to accept the life we are now living as being normal. We have moved home. Our old home held too many terrible memories. Tom is at a different school and studying for exams. The case files of Jane's misdemeanours have gathered dust in the archives and all but forgotten. They belong to a different life.

Having finally blown the tolerance of my employer I have a different job. I have thrown myself into my new job which was far simpler than my old one. I made rapid progress and have been rewarded with several quick promotions. I recall reading in a questionable US study that some employers considered the ideal employee as in their late thirties or early forties with their family life behind them, possibly divorced (or in my case widowed). Freed from distractions these ideal employees would put their effort into work. They would probably also be thinking about the future and keen to earn even more money. I fitted this model perfectly.

Of course young people wanted to earn money but there was often no real purpose behind it. Their ambition was to earn more money not do something tangible with it. What they earned they spent. If they earned more they spent more. Their financial future was not a cause for concern. They would sort it out later. Something was bound to turn up.

Forty somethings like me were planning for their retirement. They had to make a go of things in case it was their last chance. Forty something was supposed to be when we start to become aware of our mortality. Time is running out to secure the future.

I did not need to be forty something to appreciate mortality. I had seen it at first hand. I already knew how fragile life was. Mortality had screamed at me and it hurt. My own motivation was to ensure Tom would have a secure future and if that meant money then I was determined to earn sufficient.

Tom was now a typical teenager, frequently lost in his own world and morose as his brain tried to cope with the physical changes going on in his body. Each growth spurt had seen him withdraw into himself until his brain managed to gain control of his increasing bulk. Then he would come back to life and show hints of the little devil he used to be.

He has his own grown up shoes now and mine have lost their fascination. In fact he is almost big enough for me to borrow his. I would certainly treat them with a little more respect than he treated mine. I just need to persuade him to buy shoes that are more suitable for a middle aged man. I would look foolish in his fashionable designer shoes.

The toy rabbit he was so attached to got lost in the move to our new house. Perhaps it ran away fed up with the constant abuse. Fortunately Tom has grown sufficiently for me not to have tried to con him with a replacement. His interest is now elsewhere. He is more interested in gadgets. That does cause some concern given what happened but I feel unable to stand in his way. Gadgets are the normal trappings of boys of his age and I want his life to be as normal as possible. A father obsessed with the danger of gadgets would not help. And of course forbidden fruit has a compelling attraction especially for a teenager. As Angela had once demonstrated saying no was counterproductive. I convinced myself that his enthusiasm for gadgets was good; it showed that he was a normal teenager.

His boisterous energy and ability to find pleasure in the smallest things has gone. He puts up token resistance and rebels against my strictures. We have frequent stand offs as we engage in a battle of wills. I usually win but never push him too far. When I think it harmless I will concede and let him have a small victory. Even after all this time I still harbour caution. I am still wary about the lasting damage from the trauma of his early childhood.

Despite our battles I am overjoyed to see that he is a normal difficult teenager. I remember those traumatic years of my own youth when so much of life was a baffling mystery. So many things happened over which I had no control. The rest of my life lay ahead full of uncertainty. It is little wonder teenagers prove so difficult. Tom was proving difficult but for all the right reasons.

We have lost contact with Father Lucas. He was too much of a reminder. Despite his constant preaching that time was a great healer I didn't feel healed. I felt like I had endured some terrible illness that was always ticking away in the background waiting to strike again. They say we never forget anything. It is all stored in our memory. It is the retrieval mechanism that weakens as we grow older. Perhaps this is what is meant by time being a healer. Perhaps the weakening retrieval mechanism makes it appear that we are healed. Would I need to start to become senile in order to effectively erase the memory of everything that had happened? If waiting for senility is my life ambition then I really am in trouble.

I still suffer moments of depression. Angela would have been twenty one and I celebrated her recent birthday with deep sorrow. I thought of the person she could have become. Would she have gone to university? Would she have a job and if so doing what? Would she be married? Would she have a child of her own? So many questions to which there could never be an answer. Despite the futility I torture myself asking them.

Father Lucas had said Jane had a dark soul. Did this mean she was doomed to be a restless spirit unable to find peace? I do not believe in ghosts but somehow Jane lingers in my mind like a ghost.

I do not fear the night and the dark shadows. I fear the ring of the telephone or a knock on the door. I cannot rationalise these fears. I lost the ability to rationalise all that time ago. When things happen that make no sense to the sane mind there can be no rationalising. We can only try to weather the turmoil and trust that we will survive. But it changes us. We have no idea what sort of person we will be on the other side.

I have tried to learn from what happened. That we all have the capacity within us for both good and evil is undeniable. Our conscience and cultural upbringing mean that most of us choose to suppress the evil. For the vast majority of us there is some innate instinct that tells us that evil is wrong. But that instinct must be cultivated. We are taught by our parents and others around us to recognise what is right and wrong but its our own innermost thoughts that decide who and what we become.

With this learning our innate instinct develops and we start to learn from experience. Things happen to us that instinctively we know are wrong. We have a sense of injustice from an early age. In the first few years of our lives this sense is perverse. A child will do things and get upset because it is chastised. Being deprived of a sweet can seem like the end of the world. But as we grow and learn we begin to apply a balance to this sense of injustice. We cannot always have what we want. Things happen around us that we do not like but over which we have no control. We have to put a perspective on them and get on with our lives. Things that were so important as a child assume less significance as an adult.

What we must learn is that there are consequences to our actions and behaviour. Certain actions produce outcomes we believe to be wrong. This modifies our behaviour and we are able to survive and live in society. Society becomes civilised because most of us as members of that society behave in a civilised way.

At least, that is the theory. There have been evil people throughout history that see the world completely differently from the rest of us. The consequences of their actions hold no fear for them because in their eyes they are not seen as wrong. They believe that everything they do is right. Their desires and aspirations are seen as paramount and override any consideration for others. They mould the world to suit themselves whatever the cost to others. Fortunately for mankind these people are rare. The intelligence of the masses overcomes them. Consider the harm that one person did to our lives. Imagine what the world would be like if these people were the majority.

Despite my fears the dark figure did not make another appearance. Whether Tom saw him again I do not know. He never spoke of it and I never asked for fear of awakening bad memories. I did however carry the feeling that something or someone was hovering over us. We were never quite alone. There was a dark presence in our lives. Someone was watching. Father Lucas believes that our souls live forever, even dark souls. The thought terrifies me. Do I too have a dark soul lurking inside me waiting for the chance to break free? Will I meet Jane again in another life and which Jane will it be?

Lightning Source UK Ltd.
Milton Keynes UK
UKHW01f2330290518
323433UK00001B/8/P